Last
Train to
Helsingør

Last
Train to
Helsingør

HEIDI AMSINCK

MUSWELL
PRESS

First published by Muswell Press in 2018

Typeset by M Rules
Printed and bound by CPI Group (UK) Ltd, Croydon CR0 4YY.

A CIP catalogue record for this book
is available from the British Library

ISBN 978-0-9954822-4-1

Muswell Press
London
N6 5HQ
www.muswell-press.co.uk

To my mother and father

Contents

Last Train to Helsingør

As the train left Copenhagen Central Station, Henrik Borg set down his briefcase and cooled his forehead on the windowpane. He always did so at the precise moment when the platform began to glide away. He closed his eyes and let the receding lights from the station flicker across his face.

For years Borg had taken the last train home from the office. He always sat by a window and always at the far end of the last carriage, which left him with only a short distance to walk at the other end.

Tonight was like any other in all respects but one. Borg had been persuaded by a colleague to join a drinks party and had indulged in not one, but two large glasses of beer. There was a smile on his lips. His wife always said that he should be more adventurous, and now he had been, and it had passed off very well.

His initial fears about the evening had been unfounded. In fact, it had been a pleasing little break from his routine, which normally saw him working straight through from supper.

It was springtime, and they had been sitting like Parisians amidst the bustle of a square. Borg was not drunk exactly, but relaxed and at peace with the world. The carriage was warm and gently vibrating. There was a soothing, rhythmic knocking sound as it rolled along the tracks, and now and again sparks illuminated the railway cutting with a screech of grinding metal.

He supposed drinking beer was not a real adventure but it was as much as Borg could do. He did not care for fun in the way that other people did, nor weekends and holidays with their bothersome expectations of pleasure. Borg liked Monday mornings, and he liked the train. Not that he had to take public transport. He had done well for himself and could afford to drive a Mercedes to and from work. There was a parking space for each of the partners at the office, but Borg preferred the train, because it was predictable. Nothing stopped it haring through the dark as the people of the suburbs lay fast asleep. He liked the soft, warm seats, the way the plush upholstery tickled his fingers.

There were other professional types on the train. Borg nodded at them in a spirit of fraternity. Together they kept watch over the drunks and other human detritus that washed up on the late-night service. They had to be tolerated, but Borg knew that the train belonged to the likes of him: the people who kept the world spinning round.

He watched as the train cleared the inner-city stops in fast succession, always a little uneasy when it rolled into a platform. You never knew who might step in. Besides, those stops were like an invitation, as if the train itself were tempting Borg to step out and explore. He always looked at the ceiling, willing the carriage to start moving again.

His late nights at the office suited both him and his wife. By the time he got home, she was fast asleep in the spare room that she had made her own. It was an orderly arrangement, protecting their two worlds from unpleasant collisions. And his wife was more than happy for him to take his time in the mornings; she rarely stirred before midday.

The train was softly lit. In the window, Borg saw the silhouettes of houses, posts and fences passing across his reflection. The last passengers in his carriage got out at Hellerup. He could relax now until Helsingør.

Borg closed his eyes, feeling the train gently oscillating. The motion set him in mind of galloping across the plains of the Wild West, like the cowboys of his boyhood picture books. Within minutes he was fast asleep, cantering through a cartoon landscape of cacti and stone formations.

Later, the first thing he became aware of was the cold, then the utter silence. Before he opened his eyes, he felt a light on his face, which was odd, because it was completely dark all around him.

It took Borg some moments to remember where he was. 'Hello,' he said, pointlessly, for it was plain that he was quite alone in the carriage.

As his eyes got used to the gloom, Borg saw trees and bushes outside the window next to him. He got up and walked over to the other window and saw more trees further away. He looked at his watch. He had been asleep for nearly an hour, so the train must have been to Helsingør already.

He fumbled for his phone, grateful when his hand finally closed around the smooth pebble, but it had no power left. He always charged the phone before he left the office, but, of course, tonight he had gone out instead of working.

Now Borg was frightened. Something had happened, something awful, and he was unable to phone for help.

With some difficulty he managed to open the door by pulling the emergency handle. His legs trembled as he emerged onto a narrow tarmac platform, and almost buckled under him when he saw that the rest of the train had gone.

There was a wooden shelter on the platform and a post with a sign, but the name had faded and was illegible in the dark. It looked like a disused station, perhaps now deployed as a siding by the railway company. His carriage had somehow become detached from the rest of the train and left there.

If only he had never drunk those beers, he would not have fallen asleep on the train. He never had before, in all his life, and now look what had happened.

A movement at the far end of the platform startled him. It was a man slowly walking away, pushing a bicycle. A bell tinkled faintly as he went, and there was a bright light bouncing from the front.

Borg was relieved. He soon caught up with the man. 'Thank God, there's someone else here. I fell asleep. Where are we?'

The man shot him a look, more weary than unfriendly. He said nothing in reply.

Borg noticed that that the bicycle had an old-fashioned carbide lamp attached to it. Had the man held up that lamp and looked through the window of the railway carriage as Borg sat sleeping? Was that what had woken him?

The man looked odd in his worn corduroy suit. His glasses were held together with brown tape.

'Do you know this place?' Borg said, trying to keep his voice even. 'Can you tell me where I might find a payphone?'

The man shrugged. He started walking but not as fast as he could. After a moment he stopped, his face half-turned.

'You want me to follow you? Is that it?' Borg said, guessing that the man might be foreign or speech-impaired.

The man nodded once and began to walk again, this time without stopping. Borg decided it would better to follow than remain at the siding by himself.

He thought there would be houses where he could call for help, but he saw none at all. The platform ran into a narrow gravel path that led into woods. Then he and the man seemed to walk for a very long time, with only their crunching steps and the faint tinkle of the bell to break the silence. The woods smelled of leaf mould and wild garlic. Borg shivered in the damp cold. The briefcase was heavy, and he had to keep transferring it from one hand to the other

He almost cried with gratitude when finally he spotted a faint light through the branches. There were people here after all, civilisation. Soon afterwards, he and his mute companion reached a set of tall iron gates. The man got out a key and opened them, carefully relocking them once they were through. The heavy chain seemed draconian, but Borg guessed it was there for a reason. A property in so isolated a position would be vulnerable to burglary.

They walked towards a handsome white manor house, standing at the end of a long straight drive bordered by trees. As they got nearer, Borg could see outbuildings and what looked like stables. He smelled manure and livestock and, more vaguely, a salty tang. The house had to be by the sea, somewhere near Helsingør.

Up close, from the cobbled courtyard, the house looked even more impressive. Honey-coloured light streamed from several windows. Borg was lifted by the sight. He happily followed the silent man through the front door. It clanged shut behind them.

The vast, high-ceilinged entrance hall was a surprise. Borg was certain he had never seen anything so beautiful. There were trees and flowering plants everywhere, growing from large, brass pots scattered about the floor. And hanging from the ceiling and perched on stands, dozens of birdcages full of budgerigars, yellow, blue, green and turquoise, fluorescent in the gloom. When he approached, Borg saw that the birds were sleeping, heads tucked under their wings.

They keep birds. So they must be nice people, he thought.

The sound of loud voices made him turn. Two old women had entered the room, obviously roused out of bed. They wore dressing gowns and their long, silvery hair hung loose over their shoulders. Borg was reminded of his grandmother, a mild-mannered woman who had looked after him during his school holidays.

He noticed that the women's faces were identical.

'Joachim!' exclaimed one of the twins, clapping her hands. 'What have you got for us this time?'

'Yes,' said the other, stepping up close. 'What are you?'

Borg felt confused. He looked from one face to the other. 'I . . . I'm a lawyer,' he stammered.

'Oh,' said the first twin, her smile fading.

'Oh dear,' said the other with a frown. 'We already have three of those. Do you not cook or butcher or keep bees? We need a beekeeper, desperately.'

'Look here,' said Borg, trying to muster his most

authoritative voice. 'My name is Henrik Borg. I am a highly esteemed solicitor, partner of Borg, Wiesener and Bundgård. Something unfortunate happened. I fell asleep on the train to Helsingør and woke up in a siding where your good man here found me. Now would you be so kind as to lend me your telephone? I shall be out of here before you know it.'

'Oh, we don't have telephone,' said one of the twins. 'But we always welcome lost travellers.'

'I am Andrea von Trauen,' she said. 'And this is my sister Dorothea. You'll be very comfortable here with us. Everyone always is.'

Borg was astounded. 'You mean I am not the first person this has happened to?'

'Goodness no,' said the first twin.

'Though it has been over a year,' said the other. 'That's why we're so excited.'

Borg counted his options. The only thing he could think of was walking to the nearest house. In the dark and cold, this would not be pleasant. Besides, by the time he got a taxi it would be halfway through the night.

'Now,' said one of the women. 'We have a bedroom ready for you. Joachim will take you there and make sure that you have everything you need.'

'And then we will see about things in the morning,' said the other.

Yes, thought Borg, Why not? A bed for the night in the

house of these eccentric old sisters. What could possibly happen?

His wife would not miss him. And, if drinking beer after work did not amount to an adventure, this certainly did. It would be an amusing story to tell tomorrow when he was back at the office.

His room was large if somewhat fusty, with its mahogany bedstead and heavy brocades. A window overlooked the back of the property, but it was too dark to see anything outside.

Joachim, who was obviously some sort of factotum in the household, pointed to a tray with a glass of milk and a couple of plain biscuits. He hesitated in the doorway, his eyes resting on Borg's for a few seconds, as if he were about to speak. Then he was gone.

Borg sat on the bed in his underwear and socks. He drank the milk and nibbled on the biscuits, which were the kind his mother used to give him when he was little and under the weather. Their sweetness, mixed with the creamy, warm milk, was oddly comforting to Borg. He had no trouble sleeping. In fact, he was out cold as soon as he had wriggled under the heavy eiderdown.

He woke with a leaden head. The sun hurt his eyes. There were voices, whispering next to his bed.

'I agree with you, dear Andrea, that he is a not a muscular man and perhaps a little disappointing all round, but there are plenty of good uses for him.'

'All right, Dorothea, if you think so. We will put him to weeding the rose beds and then we'll see where we go from there.'

Borg sat up with a start. Judging by the bright light, it was midday already. He looked for his watch. It was gone, as were his clothes and his briefcase. The sisters, now dressed austerely in black dresses, with their hair scraped back into tight buns, stared at him with patient curiosity. There were bundles of keys dangling from their waistbands.

'What's this?' yelled Borg. 'Where are my—' But he halted abruptly, for a sharp bolt of pain had taken his breath away. It came from his neck. He felt with his hands and found a metal collar there, fastened tightly with a padlock.

'Why are you—?' Again, he was halted by a searing pain.

He noticed Joachim standing by the door and working a set of switches on a small box with an antenna, which looked very much like a remote-control device.

'There, there, Henrik,' said one of the sisters. 'Everyone is like that at first. You'll soon get used to speaking only when asked.'

Borg leapt out of bed, wondering if they would stop him from moving. But they didn't seem to mind him crossing the floor.

He looked out of the window at vast kitchen gardens and, beyond, fields with sheep and cows. He could also see a hen run, a pig sty and an orchard with fruit trees. There were people everywhere, calmly going about their work. No one spoke.

He heard the rustle of skirts as the sisters came up behind him.

'The farm was our father's, but we couldn't cope after he died. Then one night Joachim arrived, just like you did, from the old station. It only took a small amount of persuasion to make him stay,' one of them said.

'It was Joachim who thought of the collars. He used to be a science professor,' said the other. 'By the way, if you attempt to cross the boundary, you'll get a nasty shock, but there's no need for you to worry about that.'

'Think of it as an exchange,' said her sister. 'You help us, and we help you. Ours is a life of strict rules and routines. You will work and you will see the fruits of that work on your dinner plate. Each day will be the same: no changes and no surprises. You will like it, I assure you. Everyone does eventually, for what more can one possibly want from life than this, Henrik?'

Helplessly, Borg followed the sweep of her wrinkled hand. He would have said that he wasn't much good at gardening or anything else remotely practical, for that matter, but he was too frightened to speak and dared only shake his head a little.

He thought of his wife, who would be starting to wonder where he was, vaguely, before rolling over in bed with her sleeping mask and earplugs. His colleagues would joke about him being hung-over for the first time in his life. Then, after a week, they would remind each other that Henrik had been working hard before he disappeared, and that people under stress were capable of the most unpredictable behaviour, even walking out of their lives without so much as a goodbye.

No one would come looking for him, least of all in this place. No one would ever suspect the last train to Helsingør.

The Music Box

Seated in the front row of the auction room, Verner could hardly contain himself. With clammy hands he clutched his catalogue, willing the auctioneer to move faster through the lots, an endless stream of clocks and mechanical toys in which he had no interest whatsoever.

Over and over he read the description: *Rare Polyphon disc-playing music box known as 'The Schönwald', set in a hand-built walnut cabinet with latticework and painted Danube motif. Leipzig, 1875.*

Twenty-eight years ago he had sat in this same seat, only to watch Oscar Persson from Malmö outbid him. But Persson was dead now, and Verner was old, with liver spots creeping across his hands and enough money to buy anything he wanted.

He looked over his shoulder at the packed room, satisfied

to recognise no more than a couple of small-time collectors in the crowd. As he had learnt to his cost, you could not win at auction against someone willing to pay any price, and he had instructed his banker to prepare for the transfer of a very large sum of money indeed.

The Schönwald was one of the finest Polyphons ever made, a music box with a sound so pure it was said to be like listening to the angels play their harps. In over a hundred years, only a handful of people had heard it, and now Verner was about to become one of them.

There was nothing in the catalogue about the curse, but Verner knew the story. It had been all over the papers again that morning.

The Polyphon had been built on commission for Franz Schönwald, a merchant from Cologne, as a wedding present for his wife Maria. She had adored *The Blue Danube* – composed by Johann Strauss a few years earlier – so this was the only tune the Polyphon played.

According to the story, Maria listened to the music box only once, as shortly afterwards a chandelier in the Schönwald mansion dropped from the ceiling and killed her on the spot. Distraught, Franz Schönwald forbade anyone from playing the Polyphon again.

When he died, the music box passed to his nephew, whose young daughter Katharina found it in the attic and played it before anyone could stop her. Shortly afterwards, she died in a house fire.

Since then the Polyphon had passed through five owners, four of whom had supposedly died in accidents after playing it. The sixth, Oscar Persson, had kept it in a locked cabinet and never touched it, or so he had claimed.

No doubt the story was good publicity for the auction house, Verner thought to himself. But whatever anyone said, the Polyphon had not wrenched the chandelier free from the ceiling, nor struck a match and set fire to the house. It was not bad luck that killed people, but lack of care.

When, finally, the Polyphon was wheeled in front of the auctioneer, Verner had to concentrate hard not to leap up and shout with both hands in the air. In the hush that had fallen over the room, his heart was a booming drum.

As tall as a man, the top of the Polyphon was crafted in the style of a fairy-tale castle with columns and turrets and tiny windows and doors. In the centre, behind glass, sat a perforated steel disc, and on the bottom panel an exquisite painting showed a stretch of the Danube with a wooded bank, a white castle and snow-capped mountains just visible in the distance.

There were other bidders, but in the end they must have sensed that Verner would have kept raising his hand until everyone had left and the lights had been switched off, for one by one they folded, shaking their heads.

Finally the auctioneer pointed at Verner and dropped his gavel hard, and there was a gasp around the room.

As he put on his fur hat and left, Verner noticed two people get up and follow him. In the vestibule, he turned around to be blinded by a flash.

'Are you concerned by the curse, Mr Borg? Will you be playing the music box?'

Verner didn't normally speak to reporters, but on this occasion he was happy to make an exception.

'Yes,' he said. 'I shall play it and I shall enjoy it, and you shall see there is no such thing as a curse, only silly stories.'

It wasn't until he had left the building and sat in his car outside that he permitted himself the tiniest of smiles.

It was a whole twenty-four hours before the Polyphon could be delivered, and the waiting was sheer agony.

Sleepless, he got out of bed and walked through his apartment and stood by the window to look out at the city. Far below him, Sortedamsøen lay like a black mirror, ringed by street lights. Somewhere out there, the Polyphon would be standing in a dark warehouse, with a label with his name on it, and the thought of it made his heart flutter.

Twice he had telephoned the auction house to make sure they had received the money. And three times he had called the delivery people to make sure they had the correct address. So much could go wrong and Verner never left anything to chance.

To calm himself, he inspected his collection room to make sure everything was in place.

He had had a special display case built in solid oak, taking up one entire wall. Each of the more than one hundred compartments held an antique music box, from the tiniest French pocket watch to a large carousel, which had once stood in a child's bedroom in Geneva.

Verner had spent the whole day climbing up and down a ladder to dust the shelves and polish the music boxes, taking each one down and playing it before putting it back and locking it behind its glass door. Now, standing on the floor, bathed in light from an unusually bright moon, he reached for the first piece he had been given as a boy, a ballerina in a gold enamel case no bigger than a matchbox, twirling in front of a mirror. The mechanism still worked when he turned the key.

As the tiny scroll wound its way through its halting rendition of the theme from *Swan Lake*, he held the box up in front of his face, imagining that he was a giant looking in through the window, his huge eye framed in the mirror behind the dancing girl.

There was only one space left in the display, a large compartment on a raised podium at the centre. All these years it had stood empty, waiting for him to buy the Polyphon and complete his collection.

The next morning, he was dressed and out of the apartment before eight, stamping his feet on the icy pavement and peering down the road for the van. It was after nine – and he had been back up to the apartment twice to phone the delivery people – by the time it finally arrived.

'For God's sake, be careful. That thing is irreplaceable,' he said to the men as they struggled out of the van with the music box, which was wrapped in padding and plastic and fixed to a pallet.

He saw the men exchange a look as he ran ahead of them and opened the doors, telling them to mind the loose tile in the lobby and keep the music box upright and take care that their fingers didn't slip on the plastic.

The Polyphon was too big to fit in the lift, so they had to haul it up the stairs on a trolley. Verner felt a churning sensation in his stomach every time they cleared a step, setting off a faint tinkle inside the package. It took the two men almost an hour to reach the fifth floor.

Verner watched as they peeled off the wrapping, anxious for a moment that it should turn out to be a different object altogether, but in the end, there it was, the Schönwald Polyphon, smelling of furniture polish and cigars.

He made the men wear gloves as slowly they lifted the music box into place in its compartment in the display cabinet. It fitted perfectly, Verner was delighted to see, as though it had been there always.

When the men had left, he locked and bolted the front door. In the collection room, he closed the curtains and switched off all the lamps, leaving only the display cabinet brightly lit.

Then he got his best armchair and placed it on the Persian rug in the middle of the room, facing the Polyphon. He put a small side table next to the chair and fetched a decanter of Cognac and a crystal tumbler to place on it.

With a soft cloth, he gently polished the Polyphon, running his hands over the distant mountains and the broad-flowing river, before bending down and looking inside the little windows and doors.

Finally, with trembling hands, he reached into the cabinet and picked up the silver coin, which was still sitting in its little brass box from the last time the Polyphon had been played.

Once, Maria Schönwald had held the same coin in her hand, dropping it into the same slot high up on the side of the Polyphon.

When the coin had fallen with a loud clunk, Verner went and sat in the armchair, too nervous all of a sudden to drink the Cognac he had poured. What if there was something to the story after all?

Too late now. He watched the coin slide slowly down its brass runner, flick the mechanism and begin to turn the perforated steel disc with the words *An der schönen blauen Donau* written in a tall, looping script.

At the first few notes, Verner felt his heart begin to pound hard. The sound was astonishing. He closed his eyes, imagining the Schönwald's lounge, tall windows opening on to a lawn sloping down to a lake. The long curtains fluttered in the breeze and sunlight speckled the parquet floor as Maria and Franz swept across it in a waltz, her silk skirts rising and falling like a great pink powder puff.

When the tune had ended, he sat quite still and waited for several minutes. Nothing happened. The apartment was silent. He could hear the traffic in the street, a door slamming in his neighbour's flat below.

'Bad luck, my foot,' he snorted, chuckling a little at how nervous he had been.

It was just a music box after all, just wood and brass. Besides, what harm could he possibly come to, if he were to stay in his apartment from now on and speak to no one and do nothing but listen to it?

He got up, opened the music box and reached in to retrieve the silver coin.

This time he was going to enjoy it more, listen out for the little idiosyncrasies on the disc. He was going to sip his Cognac and listen to the Polyphon and glide down the Danube until it was time to go to bed, and the next day he would do it all again.

He got his fingers on the coin, but it seemed to have got itself wedged fast into a groove. He pulled at it hard, but it wouldn't come loose. He fetched a can of oil and sprayed it onto the coin to loosen it, but still it wouldn't budge, and his fingers kept slipping on the grease.

Then he fetched a pair of pliers, fixed them around the

coin and pulled till sweat began to trickle down his temples, but the coin stubbornly refused to move.

If only I can get purchase, I will be able to pull it free easily, he thought.

He placed his right foot on the bottom of the cabinet, braced against it while pulling on the pliers with all of his remaining strength.

A couple of hard tugs, and Verner fell back on the Persian rug, clutching the coin in relief.

He was still staring at it, wondering what had got it stuck in the first place, when he heard a loud crack and sensed something move and shift and slide above him with a sudden catastrophic noise.

'Oh,' he said, looking up in detached surprise, almost admiration.

I should have asked the carpenter to fix the display cabinet to the wall, was his last thought, before the air above him darkened and a mass of glass, oak and music boxes came down towards him in a great tuneful rush of air.

The Chanterelles of Østvig

The morning after the doctor told her she was dying, Gudrun Holm woke early, overwhelmed by despair for the chanterelles. The thought of them growing unnoticed in the forest after her death was unbearable.

She pushed back the covers and sat up in bed, wincing at the pain. It was everywhere now, not just in her chest. Her breaths were wheezy and ineffective, her lungs like perforated bellows.

Through the open window, she could hear the eternal sigh of the North Sea. The dawn air was damp and fragrant with rose hip and wet grass. No wind stirred the net curtains.

She snatched a whining mosquito out of the air and squashed its quivering limbs between her fingers before setting two feet on the cold floor.

Five generations of Holms had picked chanterelles in the great sand-dune plantations. She was the last of the line, the only person living to know where the chanterelles of Østvig grew.

Unless she told someone.

A stench of spoiled fish greeted her in the kitchen, last night's cod. In the end, she had not had the appetite for it. She emptied the pan outside by the woodpile. Something would eat the fish – foxes, rats, gulls.

Like her body when they finally put her in the ground, the cod would be reclaimed by nature. Nothing was wasted in the end. Even her own flesh would make a feast, if only for maggots.

She looked out over the dunes, followed a V-formation of migrating geese pulling across the flat expanse of lyme grass and heather. The sky was bigger here than elsewhere in Denmark. The deep blue light cast a primeval glow on the landscape, as though it had never been morning there before. She licked her lips and tasted salt.

The vicar picked up on the seventh ring, his voice thick with sleep. 'Gudrun. You are up early.'

'Vicar, I'm dying,' she said, brushing off his noises of sympathy. 'But that's not why I'm calling.'

'No?'

She pictured the vicar squinting beneath his great domed forehead, his hand crabbing across the bedside table as he searched for his glasses. She stemmed her impatience at his dithering. After all, he had known her as a child and would, by long-standing agreement, be the one laying her to rest in a few short weeks. There would be no mourners.

'I wish to pass something on to you,' she said. 'It's about the chanterelles. I want to tell you where to find them.' She allowed a pause for the vicar's reaction. It wasn't much.

'Oh,' he said. 'Oh, I see.'

'Well?' she said. 'Will you come with me today, so I can show you?'

When the vicar cleared his throat, she could tell that he was about to disappoint her.

'I'm old, Gudrun, and won't be long after you in Heaven. You don't want to trust me with something so important,' he said.

'But you're the only person I know,' she protested.

The vicar did not bother to contradict her. Everyone knew that Gudrun Holm disliked people.

There was a moment's pause before he spoke again. 'Then there is only one other option.'

'What?' Gudrun asked suspiciously.

'It's obvious,' he said. 'It has to be someone you are yet to meet.'

She rang off.

'Easy for you,' she spat, her voice echoing in the empty house. 'You forget this isn't exactly Copenhagen Central Station.'

She sharpened her mushroom knife standing by the sink,

soothed by the feel of its pear-shaped wooden handle in the palm of her hand. The kitchen window was greasy with sea fret. No matter how often she washed her windows, the sea always won.

After drying it carefully, she wrapped the knife in a dishcloth and placed it in the faded wicker basket that was older than herself. Then she slipped a worn tracksuit top over her T-shirt, found her battered leather walking boots and tied a multi-coloured scarf over the itchy stubble on her scalp.

The bones in her buttocks grated against the saddle as she cycled slowly up the dirt track. How many more days would she be able to do this before the rest of her strength ebbed away? Two? Three?

When she reached the main road, she looked to the left where the village houses lay like a jumble of Lego bricks on the horizon.

A car passed, a sleek black number with German plates. Østvig was not what it used to be, not since they had knocked up all those new holiday homes. Once there had been fourteen sky-blue boats fishing the North Sea from the village, a grocery shop, even a school. Now all the fishermen had cleared off, and Østvig had become a hollowed-out shell, overrun with tourists from May to October.

Someone had placed a sandwich board close to her drive. *Straight on for ice cream.* She got off her bike and kicked the sign into a rose bush, then had to hobble for a minute, holding her sore foot.

The road was empty but for a small local boy who stopped and stared at her, mouth agape, fish eyes frowning.

'What are you looking at?' she scowled, shaking her fist.

When the boy had gone, she turned right onto the main road and, after about five minutes, headed down the gravel track that cut like a ruler through the pine plantation.

The sound of the ocean was more muted here, like a distant exhalation. A wood pigeon called nearby. The air was sweet and mild and buzzing with insects.

Gudrun allowed herself a moment of self-pity that this place should be lost to her, and so soon.

Sweeping flies away from her face, she rested her bike against a silver birch and concealed it with bracken.

For as long as she could remember, she had been the guardian of the chanterelles, and what was to become of them without her? Who now would bear witness to their beauty?

Her father had shown her the almost invisible deer paths that criss-crossed these woods, pointing to the mould-coloured lichen, oak saplings and thick green moss that the chanterelles favoured. They grew low, partly covered by vegetation, like gold coins scattered on the weedy bottom of a lake.

She came to a sandy hollow, dappled with sunlight. It was one of her most reliable patches, and it took her only a few minutes to find the first chanterelle. The sight of the little golden disc made her heart leap, as though it had revealed itself especially for her.

She knelt down with flies circling her head and slid two fingers around the chanterelle. It was cool under the moss. The knife sliced easily through the stem.

Like an offering to the gods, she held the pale orange trumpet up to the light, closed her eyes and inhaled its scent of wet stone and old, sweet apples.

A noise close by startled her. She dropped the mushroom. Someone was laughing in disbelief, the laughter punctured by little gasps and screams.

'*Nej, nej, nej, nej,*' said a male voice.

Gudrun moved towards the sound, keeping her feet on the thick, slippery moss that silenced her steps, and taking care not to snap any twigs or branches. Her heart beat sickeningly fast.

Something red showed between the trees: an anorak. It bobbed up and down as the stranger darted to and fro, bending and standing.

And there was something else: the forest floor was virtually shimmering with gold. Even from where Gudrun was squatting behind a stunted pine, it was obvious that there were hundreds, perhaps thousands, of chanterelles in there.

She must have made a sound after all, because the man suddenly raised his head and swivelled around to look right at her.

He was young enough to have been her son, perhaps in his late thirties. His chubby cheeks were plum-coloured with excitement, his long, greying hair tousled and wild.

'*Hej*,' he said. Just like that, as though they were old friends.

This had a disarming effect on Gudrun. She felt herself softening towards him.

'This is unbelievable, so many. Come.' He waved. 'Come and see.'

She didn't want to, but something pulled her forward, as if by a rope tied around her waist.

As she pushed through the branches, she wondered if she was dreaming. If maybe the painkillers they had given her yesterday at the hospital were causing her to hallucinate.

Her eyes took in a rucksack, tossed aside in a patch of bare sand and next to it a clipboard with a few crumpled sheets of paper on it.

The man looked at her warmly. 'I see you have the tools of the trade,' he said, nodding at her basket. 'A fellow mushroom hunter.'

She opened and closed her mouth like a cod, silenced by his forward manner.

'Do you live locally?' he asked.

She nodded feebly.

'Then, if you don't mind,' he said, picking up the clipboard and taking down a pencil from behind his ear.

'Could you tell me where else I might find chanterelles in this plantation?'

Gudrun noticed with alarm that the papers attached to the clipboard were photocopies of small-scale maps.

'No, no, it's not like that,' the man said. 'I won't be picking them. It's purely for scientific purposes – Aalborg University.' He fished an ID card out of his pocket.

Gudrun stared at it, marvelling at the barefaced cheek of this *Torben Larsen, Research Scientist, Department of Chemistry and Bioscience.* She was still too astounded to speak.

She gave back the ID card and noticed that Torben Larsen hadn't yet picked any chanterelles but instead filled two tiny specimen containers with moss and sand.

'Perhaps it's easier if you look at the map,' he said, handing her the clipboard. 'It's local people like you who make all the difference. No amount of years in a laboratory could replace what you know.'

Gudrun thought of what the vicar had said earlier. Was this the sort of stranger he had had in mind?

'Are you fond of chanterelles?' she managed to stutter.

'Oh, yes,' he said. 'My parents used to take me hunting for them. That's what kicked all this off.'

'All this?' said Gudrun.

'I'm trying to pinpoint the conditions in which chanterelles thrive. The exact type of soil they need, the required species of surrounding vegetation and so on.

The more sites like this that I am able to study, the more I will know.'

She squinted at him. Torben Larsen had his back to the sunlight. It made his protruding ears look a luminous red, almost transparent.

'You used the word "exact",' she said. 'Of course, you must already know that there is no such thing as exact when it comes to chanterelles. They are free-spirited little things.'

'Fantastic.' He rushed over to the rucksack and retrieved a notebook. 'The way you just put that.' He repeated it to himself as he wrote: 'Free-spirited little things.'

Gudrun meanwhile looked at the map, easily picking out the main road and the neat grid of tracks on either side of it. Torben Larsen came back and passed her the pencil. 'You can outline the patches with this, if you like.'

She shook her head vigorously. 'No maps. Nothing must ever be committed to paper.'

'Right you are,' Torben Larsen said, tapping the side of his nose. 'Good point, um . . .'

'Gudrun Holm.'

'Good point, Mrs Holm. You never know what hands such information might fall into.'

She looked up at him. 'Precisely, and it's Miss Holm,' she said, before making a momentous decision.

She took a deep breath. 'But I could point them out to you, if you like?'

For a moment, she considered confiding in him that she was dying, but something stopped her, something that had been niggling away at the back of her mind, a question.

'Before I do,' she said. 'Tell me, why do you need to know so much?'

Torben Larsen looked sheepish and excited at the same time. He lowered his voice. 'I wasn't going to say anything, but I think I can trust you. One secret deserves another, right?'

'Trust me with what?' Gudrun said, narrowing her eyes.

He held up his thumb and index finger, a centimetre apart. 'I'm about this close to a huge breakthrough, Miss Holm, something that has eluded scientists for years.'

He bent down and carefully picked a chanterelle.

'Soon,' he said. 'Beauties like this will be cultivated in greenhouses and polytunnels all over the world, thanks to what I've discovered.'

The clipboard became butter in Gudrun's hands, sliding out of her grip and landing on a heap of pinecones. Her nausea returned. She waved her hands helplessly in front of her chest.

'They will be on the menu of every restaurant and on everybody's lips. They will conquer the world,' Torben Larsen said, blind to her distress.

Gudrun found her voice. It was whinging and weak. 'But

it's impossible,' she said. 'People have tried, of course, but chanterelles are too fussy. It will never take off.'

'Oh yes it will. I'm almost certain I have found a way to mimic the symbiotic relationship between these fungi and tree roots under laboratory conditions,' Torben Larsen said, his eyes shining with a strange, brilliant light.

He slapped Gudrun's back, almost causing her to fall forward. She gasped for air, hands on her knees, swallowing bile.

'I'm talking about mass production, Miss Holm, a brand new reliable food source. You will not need to pick these mushrooms ever again. You will be able to buy them in your local supermarket – fresh, tinned, frozen, freeze-dried, you name it. Isn't it great?'

He laughed, mistaking her horror for amazement, her disgust for mock disbelief.

'Stop,' she said, pressing her hands to her ears. 'In God's name, stop.'

She looked wildly around the clearing. It had started to spin before her eyes, like a gold and green wheel. But Torben Larsen kept on laughing as though he had said the funniest thing.

His mouth was full of dark fillings, she saw now, and his nails were bitten right down to the peeling, bleeding skin. There were nicotine stains on the fingers of his right hand.

Her beautiful chanterelles. Torben Larsen would take them and rob them of their rarity, the very thing that made them special. The secret of the Holms would be of less consequence than a gull's feather in a North Sea storm.

A purple dusk fell over her eyes. She gripped the mushroom knife in her pocket so tightly that it felt as though her veins would burst.

'You stupid, stupid man!' she screamed.

Torben Larsen fell heavily, still with a self-congratulatory smile on his lips. He clutched his anorak and looked down in surprise at the beetroot stain spreading across his chest. Then his eyes rolled back, starting unseeingly at the summer sky, while a bluebottle crawled across his face.

Gudrun pulled back the knife. There was a lot of blood. She wiped her boots on the bracken and buried her jumper in the sodden ground with Torben Larsen's rucksack and papers. Nature would take care of his body. Not many people crossed the woods at Østvig, and by the time he was found, if ever, she would be long dead herself.

It was only when she neared the house that her legs began to tremble on the bike. The sun beat down on the tarmac and pearls of sweat ran down the back of her neck. It was windier now and the sea was up, getting noisier as she shortened the distance between herself and the beach.

When she got home, she would have a bath, then get under the cool covers of her bed, close her eyes and never rise again.

'But what about the chanterelles?' a little voice inside her insisted. 'What will it all have been for, if you don't tell anyone about them now?'

The local boy from earlier was back, poking the lyme grass with a stick as though trying to spike fish. She slowed down and looked at him more closely. There was something singular and wilful about him, something that reminded Gudrun of herself. Again, the vicar's words came back to her.

She stopped and got off the bike.

'You there,' she cooed to him.

The boy looked up, his concentrated expression contorting into one of terror and alarm. He threw down his stick and hunched his shoulders.

'Don't be frightened,' she said, wheeling the bike over to where he stood. 'I won't shout at you this time.'

The boy looked unconvinced. He was trembling, his dirty little hands balled into fists, his wide eyes fixed on a streak of blood on her thigh.

'It's nothing. I scratched myself on a branch. But listen to this,' she said. 'There is something I want to tell you, a secret.'

The boy looked at her warily, but she could tell that he was interested. No child had ever been born who didn't like a secret.

'It's a good secret,' she said. 'The sort that people would do anything to steal from you, but you won't let them. You will defend this secret with your life, even kill for it if you have to.'

'Come,' she said and made him sit down with her on a

large white boulder by the side of the road. It was smooth and warm. She felt a great sense of peace spreading through her body.

'Now,' she said, very quietly, though only the crickets and adders and skylarks were around to hear them.

'Do you know what a chanterelle is?'

The Light from Dead Stars

The man lay on his back, his slippered feet resting casually on the threshold. One hand clutched a pipe, the other the evening paper. Were it not for his vacant eyes and the dark mess on his chest, you would almost think him napping.

Gently, Viggo Jensen unpinned the crime scene photograph, leaving a pale rectangle on the wall. He placed the photograph on top of the papers he had already stowed in the cardboard box with his chipped coffee mug and spare tie. Then he switched off the anglepoise lamp and walked over to the window.

He teased open the blinds with two fingers and looked outside. She was still there, the woman on the opposite street corner, wrapped in a thick coat and headscarf. Since five at least she had been standing there, well back from the light, stamping her feet and hugging herself against the cold.

From the way she kept looking across at the main entrance, Viggo supposed she was waiting for some arrested man to be released. No matter, it was not a night to be standing on pavements. It was the last week of January and Copenhagen was freezing.

Viggo wondered if he would ever stop doing this: noticing people out of place, the seemingly insignificant details that were invisible to others. It was an occupational hazard, he supposed, like a window cleaner condemned forever to seeing the stains on the glass and not the view beyond it.

Leif Heinemann had been shot on a winter's night, mowed down on his front doorstep. Because he was a middle-aged bachelor with no living relatives, no one complained when the police eventually had to abandon the case.

Yet, to Viggo's mind, the moment captured in the photograph had never passed. Heinemann was still lying on the parquet floor, his unseeing eyes pointed at the ceiling, the pipe warm in his hand.

Viggo had asked everyone to stand back, to give him space. If you looked closely enough at the scene of a murder, the motive announced itself. But this was different. No sign of a struggle or vengeful anger, just a single bullet to the heart.

Why? What had Heinemann done? This ordinary man

who kept to himself and never hurt a fly? For twenty-eight years, Viggo had tried to answer that question. Some would say that it had obsessed him, to the point at which he was neglecting his other cases. It had not exactly furthered his career.

A cleaning woman opened the door to his office, startled at the sight of him in the dark. She lingered for a moment, as if waiting for him to make his excuses and leave.

'I'm not done yet,' he snapped. 'For Christ's sake, can't you see?'

When she had left, he rubbed his face hard, tried to force Heinemann from his mind. After all, he *was* done, completely. He had turned every stone, looked at the case from every angle and found nothing.

He opened the blinds again. The woman had gone; the street was empty. It was almost nine o'clock, and his farewell reception had finished hours ago. He had listened patiently to the speeches, and taken receipt of a silver bowl inscribed with his name and dates of service. There was nothing left to do.

Heinemann had not been robbed, nor was there any evidence of him owing money. On the contrary, for a civil servant on a modest income, he had a healthy bank balance.

On the day of the murder, he had left work at five and walked home as usual, a stroll of some forty minutes through city streets. After a frugal supper of fried herring and boiled potatoes, he had settled down with his coffee and the paper. At ten past eight, a neighbour had heard the shot and rushed out to find him already dead.

Heinemann's apartment was unremarkable. Except, in the lounge, they had found a good telescope, the kind fit for an amateur astronomer, along with several books on stars and planets. It was an obvious hobby for an unmarried man with hours to while away. Still, the thought of Heinemann sitting behind that telescope night after night, a lonely eye pointed at an unresponsive universe, made Viggo infinitely sad.

Reluctantly, he picked up his cardboard box and looked one last time around the office that was no longer his. They had taken away his coat stand, his battered filing cabinets and the old armchair he had brought in from home. A woman detective with spiky blonde hair had been in to measure up for her own furniture. She rode a motorbike to work and looked at Viggo as though she found him amusing.

The corridor was quiet, save for the ever-present sound of two-fingered typing from distant offices. The paperwork had got worse in Viggo's time. It had got so you couldn't sharpen a pencil without filling in a form.

By the stairwell, he found the cleaning woman mopping the linoleum floor with long, even strokes. She didn't look up. Viggo envied her: to take a dirty floor and make it clean, knowing that your job was done. Police work was far less rewarding. In Viggo's experience, 95 per cent of it was pointless, made up of tasks that later turned out to have been completely unnecessary.

His mobile rang, making him jump. Still the cleaning woman did not look up.

'Detective Inspector Jensen,' he said.

It was Birgit from the switchboard, only a year away from retirement herself. He was fond of Birgit, her cheerful voice on the other end of the phone. Once, at a staff Christmas party, the two of them had messed around, and she had wanted to take it further, but that was years ago now.

'Still with us?' she said.

'Barely.'

'Good. A woman called, a Gertrud Gunnersen, said she wanted to make a statement.'

'What sort of statement?'

'She refused to say, except that it was very important.'

The name didn't mean anything to Viggo. 'Tell her to come in.'

'I did, but apparently, there's something she needs to show you. And she did ask for you personally. It's out at Frederiksberg. To be honest, I am little curious to find out what it's all about.'

'I wouldn't get your hopes up,' said Viggo. 'It's most likely nothing.'

He jotted down the address, secretly pleased not to have to go straight home to his empty apartment. With years of doing nothing ahead of him, he could spare another hour.

*

There was no outward sign of an incident at the five-storey apartment block where Gertrud Gunnersen lived. Both the street and the stairwell were deserted. With a sinking heart, Viggo began to suspect that she was one of the deranged people who confessed to crimes that had never happened.

But the woman was surprisingly normal, leaving him with even less of a clue as to why she had asked for him. Around sixty, she was trim and well dressed, with reading glasses hanging from a string of beads around her neck. Her apartment was tidy and smelled vaguely of perfume. Geranium, Viggo thought.

'Thank you so much for coming,' she said, as he set down his cardboard box in the hall. 'I was just about to have some coffee. Join me?'

While she busied herself in the kitchen, Viggo looked out of the living-room window. He knew this part of Frederiksberg well. In fact, it was only a handful of streets away that Heinemann had been shot all those years ago.

From where he was standing, Viggo could see several apartment blocks with brightly lit windows. Above the roof line, the sky was full of stars. He remembered reading that some of them were long dead, only so far away that their light had taken tens of thousands of years to reach earth. To look at the stars was to look into the past.

Gertrud Gunnersen startled him, appearing suddenly at his side. 'You were lost in thought,' she said.

'Oh,' he said, taking a seat in the sofa. 'I was just thinking that January is a good month for looking at the stars.'

She smiled knowingly. 'You can speak plainly here, inspector. You were thinking of the man who was shot dead in this neighbourhood many years ago, whose killer was never found. Am I right?'

Viggo almost spilt his coffee. 'You knew Leif Heinemann?'

'No.' She shook her head. 'He was a total stranger to me, but I gather that the case was a personal disappointment for you. I'm sorry about that.'

She pointed to a newspaper clipping on the coffee table. Viggo recognised it immediately. It was an article from a few days before, announcing his imminent retirement from the police force. He squirmed, recalling its unflattering contents. The journalist had dwelt on his connection to the Heinemann case and called it his one 'notable failure'.

Gertrud Gunnersen pointed to the article. 'It says today is your last day, so I waited for you outside the police yard. When it got late, I thought I had missed you, so I went home and called instead.'

'Ah,' said Viggo. 'It was you.'

'You saw me?' She laughed. 'I thought I was being discreet.'

Perhaps Gertrud Gunnersen was mad after all. She had read about him in the paper. Was that why she had asked to see him? Was she simply angling for a little company and attention?

'Never mind about all that,' he said, trying not to sound too unkind. The coffee, at least, was good and hot. 'I am here now. I believe you wanted to make a statement?'

'That is correct. But first, I need to tell you a story. I think you will want to hear it,' she said, carefully refilling both their cups.

Viggo felt a sting of unease at the way she held his gaze. Gertrud Gunnersen seemed completely calm, too calm for a mere lonely woman.

'When I was younger ...' she began. 'When my husband was still alive, I taught the piano here in the apartment.'

She paused and looked at him, as if considering how best to proceed. 'Are you married, inspector?'

'No.'

'But you may be able to imagine that after a while the physical side of marriage can become, how shall I put it ... predictable.'

Viggo felt his cheeks turn a deep puce. He held up his hands to stop her, but she carried on.

'Well, one of my pupils was a young man, very young, inspector. Handsome. Attentive. He came for his lessons when my husband was a work.'

'Now look—' Viggo said.

'The first letter I received was a shock. Not the money, you understand, but the idea that someone would ... I suspected my pupil, of course, but he was engaged to be married and had just as much to lose as I did.'

'Blackmail?'

She nodded. 'The money had to be left in the backyard, in a piece of old pipe, behind the rubbish bins.'

'You went along with it?'

'For a while, yes. Until one day I bumped into someone just as I was about to leave my money in the pipe. I assumed he was the blackmailer; he thought I was. We were angry. It took a long a while before we worked out that we were both victims.'

'And this man, was he someone you knew?'

She nodded. 'He was a neighbour, lived on the second floor. He never told us directly, but I'm fairly certain he used to dress up in his wife's underwear.'

'Us? There were more of you?'

'Six as it turned out, all here in number 34, all receiving the same kind of letters.'

'That's a lot of secrets.'

Gertrud Gunnersen shrugged. 'Everyone has secrets. Haven't you, inspector?'

Viggo blushed again, ignoring her inquisitive glare. 'So, what did you do?'

'We had a meeting, here in my apartment. Everyone agreed that we would not put up with it any longer. We waited for the next demand to arrive, then we took turns watching out for the blackmailer when he came to collect his money, and followed him home.'

'Him?'

'It was a man. Come,' she said. 'Now I need to show you something.'

She took him to a small, spare bedroom, at the back of the apartment. The room smelt dusty and long unused. It was only big enough for an upright piano and a single bed. Viggo assumed it was here that Gertrud Gunnersen and her pupil had had their relations.

'We rarely made it further than the piano stool,' she said, guessing his thoughts.

But Viggo was no longer listening. He was looking out of the window, his gut turning. Through a gap in a tall row of trees opposite, he could see an apartment block. It was quite some distance away, but he recognised it well enough.

Gertrud Gunnersen followed his gaze. 'I knew you would understand once you got here. You see, we're not over-looked as such, so one doesn't expect to be seen. Except if someone ...'

'He never did look at the stars,' Viggo heard himself say.

'He might have done, to start with,' she said. 'But he soon moved on to something much more interesting.'

'You shot him,' said Viggo.

'Yes. We drew lots, and I lost. Someone got hold of a gun for me, the others kept watch. It was over in minutes, then we all went back to our lives. My husband and I lived happily together till he died.'

Instinctively, Viggo looked around for something with which to defend himself. He was alone with a killer. Yet he sensed no threat. Gertrud Gunnersen's peaceful expression suggested that whatever passion had driven her all those years ago was extinguished.

'Why now? Why not own up sooner?' he said.

'Because I wasn't sorry. Everyone was better off with Leif Heinemann gone. But you ... that newspaper article ... I am not a heartless woman. It's obvious that the case has been on your mind all these years. I wanted to tell you so that you shouldn't waste your retirement wondering. Heinemann wasn't worth that.'

'And the others? What do they have to say about it?'

'Four have died and one is senile, living in a home where no one pays any attention to what she says. You and I are the only people who know.'

'And how can you be sure that I won't arrest you now?'

'I can't. But I think you would agree that it would serve little purpose.'

'Apart from justice,' Viggo said.

'Justice is a big word, inspector.'

They went through to the entrance hall. Viggo picked up his cardboard box and looked at his watch. It was two minutes past midnight: he was no longer a policeman.

A sudden tiredness overwhelmed him, as though all his years of too little sleep had caught up with him at once. It wasn't like he had imagined it to be, crossing some finishing line at the end; it was more like running out of road.

He opened the front door without another word and

left Gertrud Gunnersen standing on her front doorstep.

When he reached the street, his phone rang. It was Birgit from the switchboard.

'Oh good,' she said. 'I just have to know. What was the business with that woman all about?'

Viggo closed his eyes. Actually, he thought, Birgit was wrong. There were things in life that you were better off not knowing.

'What was what all about?' he said, reaching into the cardboard box and fishing out the photo of Heinemann's corpse. He looked at it briefly before bending down and pushing it through the grille of a drain hole.

'Well, the Frederiksberg woman who asked for you to give a statement, of course.' Birgit sounded disappointed, but she would get over it.

'Oh that,' said Viggo, picking up pace as he rounded a corner and headed for home, at last. 'Just as I thought, it was nothing, nothing at all.'

The Man Upstairs

Many years ago, before I was married, I was fortunate enough to live in one of the elegant old mansion blocks in the Copenhagen district of Frederiksberg, a stone's throw from the immaculate lawns and shaded avenues of Frederiksberg Gardens. My apartment was the envy of my friends, with its parquet floors, high ceilings and ornate cornicing, but, as so often with these things, there was a downside.

I lived on the fourth floor to the right, directly above Mrs Vonnesbech, a retired headmistress with too much time on her hands. There were a few families in the building, an air hostess who was rarely at home, and a couple of single men like myself, but Mrs Vonnesbech, who knew that I was a lawyer and worked at the Ministry of Justice, had got it into her head that she and I ought to stick together as the only people there with what she called 'proper professions'.

I may inadvertently have encouraged her by agreeing to leave my daily newspaper on her doormat in the evenings once I had finished with it. In any case, she sought every opportunity to strike up a conversation with me, and if this had seemed neighbourly at first, it soon became a source of deep resentment on my part.

Mrs Vonnesbech had many preoccupations, such as the ineptitude of the social-democratic government or the frequency of our rubbish collections, but she took a particularly obsessive interest in the man who lived in the apartment above mine. No one knew anything about Schliemann, apart from his name, which was evident from the brass plate on his door, and that he played the piano.

Schliemann had offended Mrs Vonnesbech by evading her attempts to discover anything about him.

Despite living a mere floor apart, he and I never passed one another on the stairs. Schliemann kept strange hours, often leaving or returning to his apartment early in the morning. I used to imagine that he worked as a pianist in some glamorous, smoke-filled jazz club in the city – a young man's fancy.

Certainly, Schliemann often seemed mortally tired on returning home. His tread on the stairs was slow and shuffling, as if he could barely drag himself up the steps.

Though he often played the piano late at night, I didn't

mind, as he was an excellent musician with a fondness for Chopin's preludes, and the rather mournful, meandering tunes seemed to me to go perfectly with the grand surroundings of the apartment building.

Mrs Vonnesbech, however, would talk scathingly about Schliemann, complaining that he always left the street door open, sending a chill up the stairwell whenever he passed.

'Now, now, Mrs Vonnesbech, let's not go making unfounded accusations,' I protested. 'Poor Schliemann, it might not be him at all.'

'Oh, but it is,' she said. 'And he knows I know, for he hides whenever I try to catch him on the stairs, and pretends he is not at home when I knock on his door. He never answers my notes.'

I began to loathe returning to my flat in the evenings. Mrs Vonnesbech's diatribes would leave me in a cloudy mood even on the sunniest of days. I tried to vary my times of arrival, even removing my shoes and tiptoeing past her door, but Mrs Vonnesbech never failed to intercept me.

One evening I was particularly exhausted and had resolved to confront her about her unwanted attention, but no sooner had I entered from the street than her flustered face appeared over the banister. Despite my best intentions, I found myself being dragged into her apartment.

There was a smell of dinner, and on her dining table lay scissors, newspapers and her reading glasses. My heart sank. Mrs Vonnesbech was a keen amateur historian, and

I had by then been subjected to many a tedious lecture on town planning and local dignitaries.

'Now, Mrs Vonnesbech, I've had a long day in the office and I really don't think . . .'

'Wait,' she said, pushing an old photograph under my nose. 'Tell me what you see.'

'It's a picture of our building, years ago. There are no cars parked in the street, and there's a tobacconist's where the corner shop is now. When was it taken?'

'1882. Fifteen years after the building was completed, but that's not it. Look at the windows.'

'There is something, on the top floor, there. Looks like . . . could it be someone's face?'

'Yes,' she said triumphantly.

I was confused. What was so unusual about a face in the window?

'Now look at this one from 1891.'

'The shop sign has changed, and there's a horse-drawn milk cart in the road.'

'No, not that; look at the windows again.'

'Ah yes, I see, another face.'

'No, the same face.'

'Maybe, could be, but so what?'

'Does it not strike you as odd?'

'Not especially, no. It's perfectly normal for people to be standing by their windows looking out, especially if they are waiting for someone, perhaps a spouse or a child returning home. Now if you'll excuse me, I'd like to catch the end of the evening news.'

She was dejected and I had to see myself out. I felt a vague sense of guilt in the next few weeks at having so roughly rebuffed her, for she did not speak to me in all that time, but I was also pleased with myself for having put her in her place.

Of course, no such thing had occurred. One evening, about three weeks after she first showed me the photographs, I found Mrs Vonnesbech waiting for me when I returned from work.

'You won't believe this,' she said, once more dragging me into her apartment.

On her dining table there was now a stack of books and papers. The room was unkempt and smelled of the sweat that had stained Mrs Vonnesbech's shirt under the armpits and gathered on her top lip.

It is necessary to pause here to stress how extremely unusual it was for Mrs Vonnesbech to be in such a state, and it may help to explain what followed. I have never before, and never in all the years since, met anyone as fastidious as Mrs Vonnesbech. Whether it was a legacy from her days as a headmistress, I could not say, but she had always been immaculately turned out in a blouse and skirt with well-polished, brown lace-up shoes, with her grey hair swept neatly into a bun. She abhorred dirt and untidiness, protesting with angry notes pinned to the noticeboard in the stairwell whenever some poor soul had left a stain on the stairs or a bag of rubbish outside their front door.

To find her now in this dishevelled state was alarming. She stared at me with a wild, almost manic look in her eyes, and her voice was fast and breathless.

'I spent the past three weeks at the state library looking through books. I found eleven photographs of this building, from 1872 to just three years ago. Take a look,' she said, passing me the magnifying glass.

On each of the photographs, there appeared to be a face in the window of the top floor, a pale disc with dark hollows for eyes and a wide-open mouth. The angle varied, and the features were never clear enough to tell who it was, but there was someone there, I had to give her that.

'Well?' she said.

'I admit it's rather odd. There is no way to explain it that I can think of, just one of those strange coincidences. Each time a photograph has been taken, someone happened to be looking out of exactly that window.'

'It's no coincidence, it's Schliemann.'

'Come now, Mrs Vonnesbech, Schliemann cannot be over a hundred years old.'

She stared at me through her thick spectacles till I stopped laughing. It was obvious that she had gone quite mad, a woman of intelligence having lived alone for too long with nothing to occupy her inquisitive mind.

'Now someone like you, working at the Ministry of

Justice,' she said, 'you're bound to have contacts in the police who can investigate the photographs, enlarge them, analyse and so on.'

'What?'

'Think about it,' she said. 'Have you ever seen Schliemann receive post, or a visitor? Have you ever actually *seen* him at all?'

'No, but that doesn't mean ...'

Mrs Vonnesbech was standing in the middle of the floor, her hands waving about, strands of grey hair flying loose.

'There is something about him. Something very wrong, I know it. Now if only you would ask a colleague of yours to take a closer look.'

I shook my head, but she was undeterred. 'There is another thing. I need access to your apartment to see if I can hear Schliemann up there, or somehow work a probe through the floorboards. I must know what's going on.'

'Hang on a minute.'

'It's either that, or going the other way, through the loft.'

I was exasperated and used a harsh tone with her, which I now regret bitterly. 'Now listen here, Mrs Vonnesbech. It's plain that you are obsessed with Schliemann, and I want no part of it. As far as I am concerned, he's a decent neighbour who has never done anyone any harm, whereas you have made my life a misery by forcing me to listen to your banal delusions night after night after night. From now on, I would like you to leave me alone.'

I never spoke to Mrs Vonnesbech again. What happened next is something I have pieced together subsequently, and some of it is guesswork.

It is safe to conclude that Mrs Vonnesbech did not give up on her theory, at least not straight away. I know as much, because the next day while I was at work, she dropped an envelope through my letterbox with the photographs she had found of our building. On a handwritten note, stripped of pleasantries, she had repeated her suggestion that I get them properly analysed.

A week or so later, she dropped another photo through my letterbox. I could tell that it been taken recently, as I saw my own bicycle chained to the lamp post outside. It was somewhat blurred, but Mrs Vonnesbech's point was nevertheless clearly made. There was a face in the window of the apartment upstairs from mine.

I had a university friend in those days who had joined the police when I began working at the Ministry of Justice. I would like to think now that some part of me was genuinely curious about the photographs, but mostly I wanted to rid myself of my guilty conscience at the way I had treated Mrs Vonnesbech. So I dropped the photos off with my friend at the police yard, told him there was no rush, and left it at that.

Very soon afterwards, it transpired that our apartment building needed a new roof. One day, a notice appeared in our stairwell, announcing an extraordinary tenants' meeting. As leaseholders, we were called to vote on the work, the cost of which we were being asked to share.

As a novice lawyer on a modest salary, already struggling to pay the rent on an apartment I could ill afford, this was impossible for me. I moved out the same month, and so did not attend the tenants' meeting.

I later learned, from one of the other single men in the building, that Mrs Vonnesbech, who had taken it upon herself to act as spokesperson, became incensed that Schliemann did not turn up. Everyone would have to pay their share, she maintained, with no exception. Apparently, it was all they could do to stop her from marching up to Schliemann's apartment and breaking down the door.

What exactly did Mrs Vonnesbech do between that evening and five days later when the dreadful thing happened? I had seen how agitated she had become before I moved out and would not have put anything past her, including camping out on Schliemann's doorstep.

It was the air hostess who found the body in the small hours of the morning, on returning home after a long-haul flight from the Far East. It said afterwards in the newspaper that Mrs Vonnesbech was lying at the bottom of the stairs in a pool of blood, several bones in her body broken, including her neck.

On the fifth floor, they found that the retractable ladder to the loft space had been pulled down, the hatch left wide open. The coroner concluded that Mrs Vonnesbech, a woman of some girth and advanced years, had lost her footing and fallen unluckily through the gap between the stairs. It was assumed that she had been on her way to inspect the loft in advance of work starting on the new roof.

When I read the article, I got a cold feeling all over. I knew that Mrs Vonnesbech would have been trying to get into the loft space in order to spy on Schliemann. I also felt certain she would not have lost her footing. She was as strong as a bull, a keen rower who had once been a PE teacher.

Months later, my friend from the police called me about the photographs. I had quite forgotten about them and was trying to push Mrs Vonnesbech to the back of my mind and get on with my life.

'Sorry it's taken a while,' my friend said. 'The first tests we ran were inconclusive, but I got curious, so I sent the pictures off to Germany for further analysis. Only got them back today.'

He laughed heartily. 'Very clever,' he said. 'You almost had me there. But tell me, how did you do it? How did you put that ghastly face in there, the same face, in all those photos, years apart?'

I forced myself to laugh. 'That's for me to know, and you to find out,' I said. 'Glad you enjoyed the joke, my old friend.'

I cut him off, and, to my infinite shame, never spoke to

him again. He is dead now and, for all I know, he never learnt the truth.

In all these years, I have never told anyone what happened back then, not even my wife. May God forgive me, I was, and still am, a coward. I had just embarked on my legal career, and knew full well that mysterious tales about a man upstairs who played the piano, and whom no one had seen except in photographs, would do me no favours at all.

You may ask, Why tell the story now, thirty years later?

For many years, I avoided Frederiksberg, and declined any engagement, social or professional, near the gardens or the building where I used to live. But the memory of Schliemann eventually faded, as these things do, and in time I managed to persuade myself that what happened had a logical explanation, however tragic, and now belonged safely in the past.

It was last Saturday afternoon, when, on my way to collect my wife from lunch, I found myself on the very road in Frederiksberg where I used to live. When I passed the apartment building, my eyes drifted upwards subconsciously, if only for a second, and I saw the face in the window on the fifth floor, clear as day, staring at me with dark intent, the cheeks sunken beneath the sharp, pallid cheekbones.

If you don't believe me, and you happen to be in Copenhagen, go and see for yourself. You can't miss the place; it is the most imposing apartment building in Frederiksberg. Look up at the dormer windows set into the roof, to the right of the entrance door. Schliemann will be there waiting, his face set back from the glass, partly obscured by a curtain, the dark hollows of his eyes staring out at someone or something that is never coming back.

Conning Mrs Vinterberg

Of Copenhagen, as it went past his window, Roper saw a million lights reflected in black water, a gallery of mirrors by night. There was a twisted gold spire and a curious black tower reaching into the sky like a tree root. He saw yellow buses, women pushing prams as big as barges and crowds of people slowly cycling along the pavement.

A taxi had been sent to collect him from Kastrup Airport. It was lined with carpet and felt like a warm sock. The driver drummed his fingers on the steering wheel and said nothing.

Roper was dropped outside an old building fronting the docks. It had a large wooden entranceway with a door set into it, and this door was ajar. On the other side there was a dank passage leading to an inner courtyard, its cobbles shiny with melted snow.

There were many doors, but Roper followed the instructions the old Danish lady had given him and continued straight ahead, across the courtyard, to the door furthest away. Before entering, he craned his neck to see the sky framed in a dull orange square high above him. There was the distant rumble of an aeroplane.

The lights went out on the second floor of the stairwell, and Roper was fumbling on the wall for the switch when the sound of a door being opened somewhere above him made his armpits prickle coldly.

'Come on,' he mumbled, clutching the leather satchel containing the pittance in Danish kroner that he had agreed to pay for the Chinese vase. 'You're not afraid of a little old lady now, are you?'

He felt quite sure that the vase was genuine Qing dynasty. Mrs Vinterberg had described all the markings and colours to him in great detail. Though, of course, as far as she knew it was worthless. 'A common reproduction artefact. We see a lot of them in London,' he had told her.

To Roper's mind, lying in this way was not unfair. As far as he was concerned, it was *caveat venditor*: vendor beware. Besides, ridding the elderly of their unwanted clutter was nothing less than an act of charity.

Finding the light switch, he continued upwards with renewed determination, until he reached the open door.

'Mrs Vinterberg?' he called softly on entering.

The hall had a chequerboard floor and wall lamps set into wood panelling. Roper felt as though he had stepped on board a ship, one of the old-fashioned classy liners.

'Hello? Anyone here?' he said, only to jump at the door shutting with a heavy clunk. Then came the peculiar guttural accent he remembered from the telephone.

'Mr Roper, how do you do.'

Mrs Vinterberg – a tiny, breakable thing of at least eighty – had been in the hall all along, hovering behind the door. She was dressed eccentrically in a long sequinned caftan with a turban made from colourful silks, and had mournful eyes and waxy skin.

Roper towered over her as she spoke.

'You will join me for a cup of tea, yes?'

Without waiting for a reply, she led him through to a cavernous lounge. Roper had to stop in the doorway and steady himself. On every vertical surface there were framed paintings and sketches and photographs. Oriental rugs covered the floor and there were several sofas, tables and gilded lamps. He wondered how many objects he could fit in his suitcase besides the Chinese vase.

Mrs Vinterberg had set a small table for tea and rattled the cups in their saucers as she poured. Roper took a big mouthful but almost spat it out again.

'What's this?' he said, frowning as the hot liquid slid down his throat. It had an aftertaste that was at the same time sweet and unpleasant, like bitter almonds.

'Black China tea,' Mrs Vinterberg said, smiling mischievously. 'With a dash of rum.'

'Thank you. It's . . . awfully nice of you, Mrs Vinterberg, the tea and everything.'

Roper forced a smile of the sort that usually worked on old ladies. 'Now, where would you be keeping that pretty vase of yours?' he ventured.

'Oh,' said Mrs Vinterberg, a look of regret passing over her melancholic features. 'You are in a hurry.'

'No, no,' Roper lied. 'Please forgive my impatience. I didn't mean to rush you.'

'That's quite all right, Mr Roper,' she replied. 'You want to get on, I understand.'

'All in good time,' he said, sipping his tea. 'I'm never too busy for a chat. Quite a place you have here, Mrs Vinterberg. Did you collect all these antiques yourself?'

Having spoken, Roper felt tired all of a sudden and suppressed a yawn that brought tears to his eyes, but Mrs Vinterberg didn't seem to notice. It was as though her gaze had turned inwards.

'My father bought most of them,' she said. 'He owned ships, freightliners, but they took a few passengers too. All over we went. New York, Sydney, Panama, Casablanca, Marseilles. It was a different world then. People took their time over things. I remember a long journey in the summer of 1952, bringing us from Copenhagen to Hamina in Finland and passing by Rouen, Bristol and Newcastle.

England has always been special to us Danes, because of what you people did in the war.'

Roper couldn't see what any of this had to do with him, nor why Mrs Vinterberg would want to be telling all this to a complete stranger who had merely answered her advertisement in the *Sunday Times*.

She suddenly cackled loudly to herself. 'You know, I love that thing you do in London theatres where drinks are left out in the interval and you can take anything you want.'

'You're supposed to have paid for them,' Roper mumbled into his teacup.

Having listened to the old lady for several more minutes, he began to look irritably at his watch. He had spent a good half hour with Mrs Vinterberg, but she hadn't as much as mentioned the vase. And now there was this strange tiredness, filling his eyelids with sand.

'Look,' he said, cutting off another of her rambling anecdotes. 'I don't mean to be rude, but I've had rather a long day. Do you think you could possibly fetch that vase now? I have the money right here, and then we can both get on with our business.' He patted the leather satchel.

Mrs Vinterberg sighed and put down her cup. 'Of course.'

'Not that I'm not enjoying our chat or anything.'

'No, no, you're right,' she said, but Roper could tell by the way her shoulders sloped that he had made a mistake.

'It's just that I don't get many visitors here any more,' she said 'and I don't care for being alone.'

'I'm sorry to hear that,' Roper said.

'Everyone I ever knew, who knew me, is dead.' The old lady's eyes were fringed with black-tinted tears. 'Is it so bad,' she asked 'to want a little company?'

'No, of course not,' Roper replied.

He was coming around to the view that humouring Mrs Vinterberg was the shortest route to the Chinese vase. But all of a sudden the old lady's voice changed. She leant forward and placed a cold hand on his arm.

'Stay, Mr Roper, please. Only for the night.'

Roper yanked his arm away in surprise. 'No ...'

'Then just until I've gone to sleep, please ... and I'll let you go,' she urged.

'No,' Roper said, getting up clumsily and knocking over his cup. He felt a spike of ice in his belly. What was happening to his legs?

'Mr Roper, please,' Mrs Vinterberg said desperately. 'Sit down and have some more tea.'

'No,' he shouted, making her flinch. 'You put something in it, didn't you?'

She looked up at him, too calmly, he thought. 'What do you mean? Mr Roper, are you all right?'

'You did, you did,' he said grabbing her by the front of her dress. 'You spiked my tea.'

'You are tired. Long journeys always make one dreadfully tired,' she said, waving her hands about.

She was like a bird. He looked at her diminutive wrists,

marbled with veins, her imploring eyes, and he knew at once that she was right. The flight *had* taken it out of him, and he had slept no more than two or three hours the night before.

He sat back down again and rubbed his eyes, tried to pull himself together.

'I'm sorry,' he said. 'I don't know what got into me.'

'The tea will refresh you. Here,' she said, pouring. Guiltily, he put the cup to his lips.

'Look, Mrs Vinterberg, we seem to have got off to a bad start,' he said before drinking another mouthful as she watched.

Afterwards, when he blinked, it seemed several minutes passed while his eyes were closed. He shook his head, but the room took its time to follow. It was as though the floor had started to move, gently swelling like the sea.

'It is I who should apologise,' Mrs Vinterberg said. 'I expect you want to see the vase now?'

'Yes, please,' Roper said, but his voice seemed to come from somewhere outside himself.

'It's the most beautiful vase you ever saw. An old man, a refugee, gave it to me in Hong Kong in 1955,' she said, but she was in no hurry to leave her chair.

Nattering on, she refilled Roper's cup, but this time he pushed it away. A heaviness had settled on his brain and it took an age before he succeeded in commanding his lips to move.

'Get it now,' he said, his voice low and slurred. 'Just get the vase.'

'Say you will stay and I will give it to you. You can have it in the morning,' said Mrs Vinterberg, who was far away now, as though he were looking at her down the wrong end of a pair of binoculars.

'Crazy old bat,' Roper said, managing with the last of his strength to pull himself up. He tried to seize her by the neck but she easily recoiled from his grasp, causing him to lose his balance. Something crashed to the floor.

'For the last time,' he gasped, bent over the arm of a chair. 'Give me the vase. Right now.'

'No.'

'Bloody witch. I've had enough of this,' he said and began to stagger across the oriental rugs, stuffing his pockets with Mrs Vinterberg's candlesticks and silver trinkets.

He could still make it down to the street. He would flag down a taxi, catch a late plane back to London.

But the door he went through did not lead back to the entrance hall. Instead, Roper found himself in a smaller room so full of objects that it was a while before he comprehended what he was looking at: suitcases, at least a dozen of them, stacked on top of one another; neckties divided into colour sections and pinned to a wall; toothbrushes, wristwatches and colognes neatly laid out in rows and fans; boarding cards, wallets, passports, some of them ancient-looking.

'My God, she *is* mad,' he whispered.

Weighed down by the loot in his pockets, he fell to his knees, then onto his back, as he recalled the words of Mrs Vinterberg's advertisement: *Pretty Qing vase. Copenhagen. Must be collected in person.*

Lying prostrate on a Persian rug, he noticed that the floorboards beneath him felt springy and loose. Was that where she kept them, the others who had come to buy her vase?

'They wouldn't stay,' said the tiny Mrs Vinterberg, who had come up behind him on her silent feet. 'No one ever will.'

Roper could no longer speak, not even scream. A plaintive ship's horn sounded in the far distance, as Mrs Vinterberg leant over him, her features set in a rueful frown. 'Goodbye, Mr Roper,' she said.

Between her small hands, she held a white cushion with the words *Baltic Marine Conference 1957* embroidered in navy blue. Roper, who by now could move only his eyes, turned his gaze to the window as she slowly extended the cushion towards his face.

He fancied he could see the velvet water of Copenhagen harbour with the million lights reflected in it, but it could have been the sky, shimmering with stars.

He closed his eyes and in a dream – his last – he saw Mrs Vinterberg come towards him on the wooden deck of a ship, a Chinese vase held aloft in her outstretched hands. The porcelain was the blue-tinged pearly white of a child's first tooth, the motifs and markings just as she had described them. It was indeed a vase of extraordinary beauty, and he reached for it, almost touching it, as dozens of Danish banknotes slipped from his hand and flew up on the wind, blackening the sky.

The Night Guard

Saturday was Leif's day for visiting the art gallery, but they had called in the morning from his mother's nursing home, and he had been forced to spend the entire day waiting for her to die, another false alarm.

By the time he finally made it to the gallery on Sunday afternoon, he was impatient to enter. The staff on the door knew him, so there was no need to show his member's pass, but he did so anyway, flashing it high as he sailed past the long line of tourists fumbling with their tickets.

It was a drizzly, miserable winter's day, but as soon as he was inside, his damp trench coat safely stowed in the cloakroom, it might as well have been summer. The rooms were warm and softly lit, enveloping him like a comforting blanket. It was as though he were strolling through one of the gallery's sun-drenched Golden Age paintings, along a dusty track towards a pleasant village.

Nodding at guards who stood at the entrances to the rooms, he began as he always did, not at the beginning, but with the nineteenth-century portraits in the furthest room on the second floor. With his hands clasped at his back, he walked, stopped, walked, stopped, taking in each of the familiar faces and scenes.

Before leaving the room, he tipped his imaginary hat at the portrait of the man he had always thought of as 'the Duke', a curly-haired nobleman on the edge of a merry group of revellers in a Mediterranean street. The women in their brightly coloured shawls, the beggar children, and the lights of the tavern up ahead offered plenty of distractions, yet the Duke alone stared out of the picture, directly at the gallery visitor. By some clever trick, his naked gaze appeared to follow you around.

Leif always skipped the sculpture rooms, finding the bronzes and marbles pointless when there was a whole building of Technicolor canvases in which to lose himself.

How stormy the seascapes looked, how bold and stirring. He sat, as he always did, for half an hour on the leather couch in front of an enormous painting depicting a sea battle. He admired the way the artist had hinted at the sunlight breaking through the smoke at the head of the fleet. When he closed his eyes, he thought he could hear it: the shouts from the men, the tumultuous waves, the cannons echoing between the great walls of the battleships. And was that not the finest web of sea spray on his face?

At four precisely, he took tea in the café beneath the stone arches in the basement, and if it were less busy than usual, he was oblivious, preoccupied by a particularly good almond pastry.

By half past four, he was back upstairs, striding out among the paintings of landscapes and domestic scenes. He always kept them till last.

The landscapes, mostly French and Dutch, were luminous and alive, not like paintings at all, but like windows onto a sunnier world.

He lost himself for a long while in a simple picnic scene under a leafy canopy by a river with a golden meadow in the background and, in the far distance, a mountain range with a road leading tantalisingly away. There was much to commend. The perfect composition of the three people in the scene. The coy demeanour and loose clothing of the ladies. The way the man looked away at the river, amused by something that would for ever remain a secret.

It must have been just before five that Leif felt the effects of the tea and got up reluctantly to head for the men's room.

Had there been an announcement while he was in there? Perhaps when he used the noisy hand drier? Later he supposed there must have been, but all he remembered was the elation he felt upon coming out and finding the long gallery with the leather couch at its centre completely empty.

How satisfying a visit it was turning out to be, he thought, as he sat down and made himself comfortable. They had even dimmed the overhead lights, a very good idea, on which he would make sure to compliment the management at the next opportunity. He was happy to note from his wristwatch that he had almost a full hour left before he had to walk through the sodden, grey city to his empty apartment.

For a long time, he devoted himself entirely to his favourite painting in the gallery. It was always reassuring to find the woman still there, feeding geese from a stable door at dawn. How carefree she appeared, despite her obvious poverty, lost in inconsequential thought as one hand scattered the grain, and the other dug deep in her apron for more. A little distance away was a charming tumbledown cottage and, through the open door, you could just about glimpse a man fast asleep in an alcove bed. Leif guessed it must still be warm from the woman who had left it.

At ten minutes to six, thoroughly satisfied with his afternoon, he began the long walk through the gallery to the exit, meeting no one on his way.

At the cloakroom desk, he frowned on seeing that the girl who took his coat had left her station several minutes before the hour. He made a note to complain about this, already feeling a pleasant frisson at the prospect of standing up to speak in the wood-panelled room where members were treated twice a year to a glass of wine and a question-and-answer session with the gallery director himself.

It wasn't till he reached the gift shop that Leif felt a stab of unease. The shop with its rows of postcards and trinkets was dark, and there was no one behind the till. He frowned at his watch. It was still not six. Why would they have closed the shop before the gallery?

By the exit he stood for a moment and scratched his head. The door was not in its usual place, or rather there was no door, merely a steel plate covering the entire opening where the door would have been. He pushed at it cautiously, to no avail. There was a red button to the side, but when he pressed it nothing happened, and he saw that it was operated by a key, and that the key was nowhere in sight.

A cold feeling came over him. He remembered now that the gallery closed an hour earlier on Sundays. He was trapped inside.

For a few seconds, a minute at most, Leif lost possession of himself. He hammered on the steel plate and screamed at the top of his voice: 'Help! Someone open the door. Help me!'

He made a terrific racket. The noise echoed around the vast hall, but nothing happened and no one answered him.

He looked around for a telephone but saw none. He patted his pockets in vain, for he had left his mobile phone at home, not wishing to be disturbed by the staff at his mother's nursing home for the few precious hours that he was going to spend at the gallery.

There was no alarm button, nothing that could be used in any way for communicating with the outside world.

It's all right, he thought, trying to regain his composure. There will be a night guard, and he will let you out. In the meantime, you will not starve or die of thirst. There are plenty of shortbread biscuits and boiled sweets in the gift shop, and you can drink water from the tap in the men's room.

He calmed down at the thought of how he would make his complaint at the members' evening: stoically, but leaving no doubt as to the horror of his ordeal.

For an hour or more, he walked at pace through the dingy rooms, astonished at how different the gallery felt now.

He called out, trying to stop himself from breaking into a run. He barely noticed the paintings now, all pleasure from them gone. As he reached the portrait room, he sensed the Duke observing him mockingly but could not find it in himself to look.

Unless he and the night guard had persistently missed one another, it would appear that Leif was entirely alone in the gallery. There was nothing for it but to wait for someone to arrive in the morning.

He returned to the Dutch landscape paintings and sat down and stared at the simple woman feeding the geese till his heartbeat slowed. The room felt colder now. Perhaps they turned off the heating at night?

After a while, he lay down on the couch, and eventually managed to fall asleep, exhausted and hoarse from the shouting.

It felt like it had been no more than minutes when something woke him. There was a noxious smell. Turpentine, he thought, his nostrils wrinkling. He opened his eyes and blinked at the vast room, trying to make sense of it. Then he remembered where he was and sat bolt upright on the couch. He immediately recoiled. There was a man standing nearby, a man wearing a black suit, a white shirt and a slim black tie.

'Thank God, you have come,' Leif said. 'Where were you? It was dreadful. They locked me in, and there was no alarm button and no telephone. I was unable to call for help. Of course, I shall have to file a complaint.'

He had got himself off the couch, somewhat creakily, brushed down his suit, which was terribly creased, and started to move off in the direction of the exit, but the night guard had not moved nor spoken at all.

'Well, come on, man,' Leif said. 'Let me out.'

The words rang out between them, but the night guard did not move. Finally, the man cleared his throat and spoke in a tired and thin voice.

'I can't.'

'What do you mean?'

'The gallery gets locked at night. There is no way in or out. You have to wait until tomorrow morning.'

Leif looked at his watch. It was only just after midnight. There would be at least another eight hours to wait. He took a step closer to the night guard, assuming his full height.

'Now listen to me. I am a member of this art gallery,' he said. 'In all my years of coming here, I have never known impertinence like this. I can assure you, my good man, that this is not the last you will hear of it. Now use your key and open the door at once, or you will be in even greater trouble than you are already.'

Still the night guard stood his ground.

'I demand that you let me out this minute!'

But the guard shook his head, looked at his feet and smiled sadly. There was something familiar about him that Leif could not put his finger on. He noticed that the man had an untidy beard and long curly hair gathered in a ponytail. Obviously, the gallery did not feel it necessary to be strict on the grooming of its night-time personnel. Well, they were wrong about that.

Leif stepped a little closer to look for a name badge on the man's jacket, but there was none. He noticed there were stains on the lapel, and on the man's trousers and shoes.

'Is that ... paint?' he asked, astounded.

He thought again of the smell of turpentine that had woken him. The night guard was standing rather close to the painting of the woman and the geese. Almost close enough to touch it.

Leif narrowed his eyes. 'What's going on here? Have you been messing with the paintings? Why that's ... that's vandalism. It's a criminal offence.'

The man shook his head with an exaggerated movement. 'No, no, not vandalism, improvement.'

'Improvement? I never heard anything so absurd.'

'All the little people in these paintings, no one knows them,' said the guard, nodding at the pictures in the gallery – the peasants, the lovers, the dead sailors and the townspeople.

Leif was losing his patience. 'And what have they got to do with anything?'

'I mean that no one knows them, except me.'

Leif stared at the man uncomprehendingly.

The guard smiled. 'All the people that come to the gallery, I put their faces in the pictures. Only takes a little, the lightest of touches.'

'I don't believe you,' Leif said. 'It's preposterous. You could not have done such a thing without being discovered. People would know.'

The guard smiled again, as though Leif had paid him a compliment. Why was the man keeping his hands behind his back? What was he hiding?

Leif leapt forward, intending to snatch at the guard's sleeve, but the younger man was faster, taking a few steps backwards and causing Leif to lose his footing. Then he turned and ran, but in his hurry dropped something on the floor.

Leif bent down. It was a paintbrush. The tip left a vermilion smear, like blood, across his palm.

For almost an hour, he looked for the guard. He searched the lavatories, the gift shop and the basement café. Once he thought he saw a glimpse of the man's ponytail at the end of a gloomy corridor, but he was gone before Leif could catch up.

Around two in the morning, he wearied, returned to the leather couch and lay back, staring at the ceiling, to rehearse his complaint. Given the grave circumstances, he thought that, as well as a speech, a written report would be appropriate, delivered by hand to the gallery director.

The cleaners found him in the morning, wound into a tight coil, a streak of saliva staining the leather.

However warranted, it was difficult to assert one's authority with day-old stubble, a crumpled suit and stale breath. Leif hadn't thought of that.

The gallery director, who had been fetched to deal with the situation, was most apologetic, wringing his hands, and protesting that nothing like it had ever happened before. But Leif could tell that the man and his embarrassed entourage wanted rid of him.

Before he knew it, a taxi was parked outside the entrance waiting to take him home free of charge as a token of the director's sincerest apologies, along with a life membership of the gallery, worth thousands of kroner.

'Now,' said the director, shepherding Leif towards the waiting car. 'I'm sure that, as a friend of our gallery, you will not find it in the best interests of such a venerable institution to speak to anyone about this . . . unfortunate incident.'

'Wait,' said Leif, trying to remove the director's firm hand from his shoulder.

The complaint was not at all turning out as he had intended; everything was coming out in the wrong order. 'I insist that you sack that horrible man. Refused to let me out, or call for help. And as for that nonsense about putting faces into the paintings . . .'

'What man?' said the director.

He was so close that Leif could smell his aftershave and freshly laundered shirt. The man's nostrils flared faintly.

'Why, the night guard, of course,' said Leif. 'His uniform was stained, and his hair unkempt. Even at night, there ought to be standards.'

The director smiled overbearingly, the way Leif had seen the nurses at the home smile at his mother, who no longer knew her own name.

'We don't employ night guards any more. Not since we installed these modern security doors, digitally controlled, and one hundred per cent reliable. No one enters; no one leaves,' the director said. 'Now, you have obviously had a terrible shock, and I doubt you slept much. Let's get you home. What did you say your address was again?'

There was nothing for it but to go home and forget it ever

happened, Leif thought. No one here would believe him anyway. He was just a visitor, a nobody.

Remembering something, he twisted himself free of the director's grip and ran back into the gallery.

'Back in a moment,' he shouted at the astonished director and his attendants. 'I forgot something.'

He ran all the way to the furthest gallery on the second floor and the nineteenth-century portraits. No sooner was he through the door than he felt the Duke's eyes on him, a little sad, almost apologetic. His curly hair was loose, the beard trimmed, but it was the night guard all right. The man had painted himself.

Henning could hear footsteps and voices approaching, but there was one more thing he had to do. He ran back downstairs and found the painting of the woman feeding the geese. He leant in close with his eyes next to the canvas and peered at the man sleeping inside the cottage with the door open. The face was no larger than the nail on his little finger, but Leif recognised himself instantly from the long nose, the white eyebrows and the slightly protruding forehead. He looked happy, at peace, as though nothing could ever worry him again.

'Is there a problem?' said the gallery director, who had finally reached him with his minions, panting from the exertion.

'No,' said Leif, turning and covering the painting with his back as best he could. 'There's no problem at all.'

The Bird in the Cage

Erik stopped in front of the shop in Christianshavn to look at the bird in the cage. It had caught his eye as soon as he turned into the road, impossibly exotic on its black velvet cushion, lit by a single spotlight. There was nothing for it but to dismount from his bicycle and stare, his face bathed in the soft yellow glow from the window.

The cage was golden with a domed roof and a square base decorated with a garland relief. Inside, on a perch wrapped in silk flowers, sat a stuffed bird, dull brown with a grey chest and rusty tail feathers.

Erik looked up and down the street. No one else was stopping or giving the window a second glance. The bird seemed to be looking directly at him, its head cocked to one side, its beady eyes fixing him with an imploring stare.

When he got to the office, he found that he could not

concentrate on anything. In meetings, his mind drifted constantly to the bird. As soon as he could, he cycled back to the shop, relieved to find it still there in the window. Standing in the dark, with the bird's huge eyes on him, he felt a quickening in his blood that he could not account for.

He thought how he should like to polish the cage till it shone, remove the faded silk flowers and replace them gently with sprigs of cherry blossom from the park opposite his apartment. He saw himself reaching in and cupping the bird gently in one hand and, in his fantasy, its tiny heart fluttered and its beak scratched his palm.

He had never bought anything for himself that wasn't in some way practical, but he knew, with a certainty that grew day by day, that he wanted the bird in the cage. He even thought of the perfect place for it in his apartment: the little window nook with the round mahogany table that had been his mother's. If the bird were his, he would pull up a chair and sit there all day and look at it as the sunlight passed through the bars of the cage and painted patterns across the floor.

The next day, he parked his bicycle by the shop, removed his helmet and smoothed down his hair. An old-fashioned bell rang when he entered, his hand moist and trembling on the door handle.

The shop was warm and smelled pleasantly of cigars and old wood. A grandfather clock was ticking loudly, drowning out the noises from the street outside. Erik stood for a while, adjusting to the dim light and the distinct sensation of having stepped outside of time.

The few objects in the shop were displayed on plinths of varying height, each brightly lit. He saw a music box with a twirling ballerina in a pink dress, a porcelain vase decorated with flowers and dragons, a tall ship with its sails unfurled inside a bottle.

'May I help you?'

The shopkeeper startled him: an old woman, tiny and stooped in a knitted black dress with thick grey stockings and black lace-up shoes. She looked up at him shrewdly, reminding him of the little brown bird with its cocked head.

Erik straightened his back, cleared his throat and spoke as commandingly as he could.

'The bird in the cage, in the window. Can I see it?'

The shopkeeper smiled indulgently. As she pulled back a velvet curtain and leant slowly into the window display, Erik fought an urge to push her aside and do it himself.

But then he saw something he had not noticed before: a large brass key protruding from the base of the cage.

'It's an automaton,' the shopkeeper said, following his gaze. 'A mechanical nightingale made by master craftsmen in Paris one hundred and fifty years ago. They used the feathers and beak from a real bird. Watch.'

She turned the key a number of times and let go. The bird began to nod its head and turn this way and that, singing trills that sounded surprisingly real, with only the faintest rhythmical clanging of the cogs below.

They stood in silence and listened. Erik thought it was the most astonishingly beautiful sound he had heard in his life.

The shopkeeper spoke softly, as though imparting a secret. 'The nightingale is celebrated for its song. It's the virtuoso of birds – few can match its range. You are familiar with the Hans Christian Andersen fairy tale?'

Erik nodded. He remembered his mother reading the story to him when he was a boy. As the shopkeeper retold it, his eyes never left the bird.

'When the emperor of China hears of the plain nightingale with the beautiful voice, he orders it to be brought to his palace. But soon his head is turned by a wind-up bird studded with jewels, sent to him by the emperor of Japan. While no one is looking, the real nightingale flies out of a window and returns to the forest. The emperor is angry and bans the bird from his kingdom. Years later, when the artificial songbird has broken, and the emperor lies dying, the nightingale flies back to the palace and sits on the windowsill and sings. Even Death is moved by the song, which makes him long for his own garden and leave the emperor's bed. The emperor lives and the nightingale is free.'

'Could you make it sing one more time?' Erik said, his voice croaky and thick.

As the bird sang again, twisting and turning its little head, his eyes filled with tears.

The birdcage did not have a price tag on it. There were no prices on any of the items in the shop, come to think of it.

'How much is it?' Erik said.

The shopkeeper looked at him for a while before replying. When she spoke, the price she gave was almost the same as the new bicycle Erik had planned to buy. He was astonished.

'How can an old thing made of a little brass and few feathers and cogs cost so much money?'

The shopkeeper gestured around the room. 'The value of these objects hinges upon the desire of customers to own them, not the materials they were made from. If someone wants something enough, no price is too high, and they will stop at nothing to get it.'

'Rubbish,' Erik said. 'People have more sense than that.'

The shopkeeper said nothing in reply, merely smiled at him and waited.

Erik thought, I want the bird, but I really need a new bicycle. I don't *need* the bird.

A shadow of these deliberations must have crept over his face, because before he knew it, the shopkeeper had gently picked up the birdcage and returned it to the window. Not knowing what else to do, Erik thanked her, left the shop and went home.

When he woke the next morning, he knew that he had

been wrong. He needed the bird more than he needed a new bicycle. A few minutes after nine, he was on his way to Christianshavn, pedalling hard.

He almost fell through the door to the shop.

'I have changed my mind,' he shouted, holding up his wallet. 'Please can I buy it, the bird in the cage?'

'Certainly.'

The shopkeeper did not seem surprised to see him. She went over to the window with no particular urgency, leant into the display and picked up the cage. Then she put it on the counter and rang it up on an old cash register Erik hadn't noticed before.

When the price came up, Erik thought there must be some mistake. The price was higher than the price of the new bicycle; it was almost as much as the new bathroom he had planned to buy.

'That's not the price you told me yesterday!'

'No,' the shopkeeper said. 'You didn't want it as much yesterday as you do today.'

Erik left without thanking her and walked all the way to the office, too miserable to even get on his bicycle.

That evening when he got home, the apartment felt even emptier than usual. He pulled up a chair and sat and stared at the round mahogany table where he had imagined putting the birdcage. It was as if it had always been there, but was now missing, leaving an empty space that could not be filled with anything.

Lying in bed that night, he resolved to go back to the shop the next morning and pay whatever the old woman asked of him. He fell asleep relieved, his mind made up.

When he stepped through the door to the shop, he was whistling cheerfully, stepping aside to make way for another man just leaving with a large box tied up with string.

'It's all right,' he said to the woman. 'Whatever the price is today, I will pay it. I want that bird more than anything. I am certain of that now.'

'I see,' the shopkeeper said, smiling that incongruous smile of hers, but she didn't move from behind the counter. 'I am afraid I must disappoint you. I just sold it to that gentleman who left the shop as you came in.'

Erik felt his knees give. He had to put a hand on the counter to stop himself from falling over. In his rush to get to the shop, he had not noticed the cage was missing from the window display.

'How could you?' he heard himself say. 'That bird was mine.'

The shopkeeper shrugged. 'The other gentleman was willing to pay what I asked. He obviously wanted the bird more than you did.'

Erik felt his hands bunch into fists. 'No one wants that bird more than I do,' he said.

The shopkeeper watched him passively as he turned around and tore open the door, rattling the bell.

He ran up the street, propelled by a force of anger he had never known before. He wasn't really there, but for his feet pounding the pavement and his fists swinging like clubs from his elbows. He saw nothing but the man up ahead, carrying the birdcage away. The long years stretched out before him, empty years of cycling to and from work and never again hearing the song of the nightingale.

He caught up with the man by the canal. He was clutching the box to his chest and shaking his head, as Erik stepped in front of him. The man's lips were moving, but Erik could only hear his own laboured breathing and the blood rushing in his ears. He grabbed at the string and tried to pull the box away from the man, feeling the birdcage moving inside. The man bared his teeth and tried to shift his grip on the string, but as he did so the box slipped from his hands and fell onto the cobbles between them; there was a loud rattling nose and a single heart-rending tweet could be heard from inside.

Something dark descended on Erik's vision then. A roar filled his head and he saw his hands dart out from his body like pistons, shoving at the man's chest. Now the man was stumbling, his arms were flailing. Then he was gone, over the edge and into the canal with a loud splash, and Erik was kneeling on the cobbles, rocking back and forth with the nightingale in his arms.

A woman's scream woke him. He felt strong arms pinning him to the ground, heard himself say, again and again: 'I don't know what came over me. I don't know what happened.'

By the time the police got the man out of the black canal water, he was dead. He had hit his head on the edge of a boat, fracturing his skull.

They put Erik in handcuffs and made him sit in the back of the police car. An officer sat next to him, holding the cardboard box in his lap as the car began to edge its way through the crowd of onlookers.

'That box is mine,' Erik said. 'Will they let me keep it in prison?'

The officer shook his head. 'If and when you are convicted, it will go into storage for safekeeping until you are released.'

Good, Erik thought and he saw himself, years from now, reaching into the squashed and dented cardboard box, gently lifting out the birdcage and stroking the little bird, and he felt calmer.

When they passed the shop window, he noticed that the birdcage had been replaced with a white rocking horse, its shiny grey mane caught in the light from a single spotlamp.

Erik couldn't help but admire it, and he turned his head to look out of the rear window of the police car. As he did so, he saw the shopkeeper standing behind the door, looking at him, seeing everything, and he wasn't sure, but he thought the old woman might have been smiling.

The Miracle in Dannersgade

When, aged seven, Lilian decided to become an organist, she had never sat at a piano, nor yet grown legs long enough to reach the pedals, but this was how she was: once Lilian set her mind to something, it happened.

It was autumn and twilight when, on her way home from school, she first noticed the peculiar old building in Dannersgade, squashed in between two apartment blocks covered in graffiti. There was a tree outside in a small, cobbled courtyard behind iron railings, and the foliage on the tree was flaming orange and red, like the burning bush in the Bible that her teacher had made them draw at school.

The door was open. Inside someone was playing the organ and the sound was catastrophic, like glass shattering, or rocks tumbling down a mountainside. It gave Lilian the strangest feeling, as though she was going to cry but wanted to laugh at the same time.

Years later, she learnt that the church had been built at the time of King Christian IV, when Dannersgade was nothing but mud and grass, but back then, as she stood by the door and listened to the music, it seemed to have come into being in that moment, especially for her.

She went in, cautiously, and stopped just inside the door, craning her neck at the vaulted white ceiling high above. The light was golden, shining from the brass chandeliers and reflecting in the candlesticks on the altar and the smaller candleholders at the end of each pew. There was a large, three-panel oil painting behind the altar, showing the Last Supper, a gilded pulpit topped with a crown suspended from the ceiling and, on the wall, the crucified Jesus, life-like and devastating in his crown of thorns.

I am the light of the world. Whoever follows me will not walk in darkness, it said in large golden letters on the pulpit.

Lilian, whose life till that day had been spent in a cramped apartment and a run-down council school, had never before seen anything as beautiful as the church. It hit her, not like a beauty you see with your eyes, but one you feel with your stomach. She dropped her schoolbag on the stone floor, and the sound echoed around the vast room.

The organist must have heard her, for he stopped playing, turned around on his stool and looked at her with open curiosity, a thin man with unruly red hair and a red beard.

He beckoned her over. She hesitated, as she had learnt by bitter experience in the neighbourhood to stay clear of strangers, but the man looked too fragile and breakable, with his pale, freckled skin, to constitute a threat.

Standing by his side, the pipes towering high above them, Lilian let her eyes roam over the three manuals, the carved wooden surround and the bewildering array of buttons with tiny letters and numbers that she could make no sense of. The organist wore long, narrow shoes. A pair of brown lace-up boots stood to one side along with a worn leather satchel from which sheets of music were protruding.

He smiled. 'Would you like to try?'

She climbed onto the stool and put her fingers on the keyboard. The sound she made was terrifying.

The organist laughed. 'You need to learn to control the beast,' he said. 'Think of it like taming a dragon.'

She looked at the organist, and behind her at Christ and the glorious nave with row upon row of painted pews, and understood in an instant that playing the organ meant he could be in this wonderful room whenever he wanted.

'Will you teach me?' she said.

He laughed again, but saw, as people soon did with Lilian, that she was deadly serious. He told her to learn the piano, and to come back when she was able to reach the organ pedals with her feet.

There were no instruments at home, and no money for lessons, so she taught herself on the old upright piano in the gym hall at school, spending hours there after lessons until the janitor chased her away.

After five years, when her legs had grown long enough, she began to take lessons with the organist, whose name was Lasse, and after seven years she could play anything he put in front of her. By then she was excellent: Lasse said that when she was playing Bach it sounded like she had four hands.

On her nineteenth birthday, he gave her a pair of red organ shoes. He had aged by then, and his hair and beard had turned grey, but still he was showing no sign of wanting to retire.

'You are ready to apply for your first position,' he told her, passing her a newspaper in which he had a circled a couple of ads from churches in West Jutland that were looking for organists.

Lasse understood nothing. Lilian did not want to play in any other church than Sankt Lukas Kirke. Whenever she turned on the organ and heard the pipes breathe, like a slumbering giant, she felt a surge of happiness. Sitting on the stool, her red shoes moving across the pedals by themselves, the music flowed from her fingers like water.

She loved the way the rain on the stained-glass windows drew patterns on the ceiling, the cool, damp feel of the thick walls against her hands when they were hot from playing. She loved the smell of wood smoke and wax, the way her little finger fitted perfectly into the grove on the underside of the third pew on the right. She loved that sometimes, when she lost herself in the music, she sensed the ghosts of worshippers past flicking across the rear-view mirror mounted above the music stand.

Above all she loved the figure of Christ, though she would not have been able to explain why. She could spend hours looking at him, waiting for him to move, to cry out or raise his head and speak to her, but he never did.

The situation was desperate. Lilian had learnt everything there was to know about playing the organ; she no longer any reason to come to the church. But the thought of not spending every day there was unbearable.

She knew Lasse cycled to the church from another part of Copenhagen. One day, while he was busy playing during the Sunday service, she snipped the brake cables on his bicycle with a pair of pliers that she had stolen from the basement under her apartment building.

Lasse fell badly, breaking both his arms in several places. Lilian threw the pliers in the lake on the way to visiting him in the hospital.

'Don't worry about a thing,' she whispered in his ear as he lay sedated. 'I will look after the organ now.'

For ten years, Lilian lived a perfect life, taking the large wrought-iron key and letting herself into the church whenever she wanted.

With the thick doors closed, no one outside could hear

her play. It thrilled her that while she filled the vast room
with the thousand voices of the pipes, people in the street
went about their dull, everyday business, oblivious.

The Sunday service, on the other hand, was a burden to
be borne. If anyone had asked her, Lilian would have said
that she did not believe much in God.

The vicar had done nothing to persuade her otherwise.
He was a disappointed man, bent over like a question mark in his black cassock and white piped collar.
Whatever he had imagined during his theology studies at
the University of Copenhagen that ministering to a flock
of inner-city souls would be like, reality had fallen short
of expectations.

When, over the years, the worshippers dwindled in numbers and people went elsewhere to marry and christen their
babies, he took his frustration out on the few blameless
souls who still came.

It got so that only a handful of deaf, elderly ladies turned
up regularly for Sunday service, so it was a surprise to
no one when Sankt Lukas Kirke found itself on the list
of Copenhagen churches threatened with closure by the
Ministry of Ecclesiastical Affairs. If attendance did not
improve, they were told, the church would be turned into
a community centre.

Lilian imagined the pews full of mothers and screaming babies. She saw how there would be yoga classes in the
chancel, hideous modern art mounted all around the walls

of the apse, and small children touching her beloved organ with their sticky fingers.

Word soon got out in the homeless shelter around the corner that Lilian bought beer for anyone willing to snooze in the pews for an hour on Sundays. For a while, the church was half full, but organists are not well paid, and soon her money ran out and the church was almost empty again.

But Lilian wasn't prepared to give up.

Looking through the vicar's files, she found the names and addresses of elderly parishioners, and began to go around an hour before Sunday service to escort the hard of walking to the church with their wheelchairs and Zimmer frames on the promise of coffee and biscuits in the church hall afterwards. While exhausting, this was a good and cheap solution until, one by one, the parishioners died off and there was no one left to bribe.

And so the dark day came when, as she set her fingers to the first chord of the prelude, she saw in her rear-view mirror that every single pew was empty.

When it came to the opening prayer, the verger stayed silent.

'That's it,' he said, slamming his prayer book shut. 'It's finished; we will have to close now.'

'Give it time – some people might turn up,' Lilian pleaded.

But it was too late. The vicar had turned round from his kneeling prayer by the altar and discovered what was happening.

His reaction was unexpected: he threw himself down on the floor in prostration before Jesus and the Apostles on the altarpiece and howled like a wounded animal.

'God, why have you forsaken me?' he yelled.

Lilian and the verger looked at each other, perplexed.

'Answer me!' shouted the vicar. 'For once, answer me.'

At that moment the chandeliers dimmed briefly, casting the church in shadows, for it was a dark winter's day. The vicar immediately stopped his bawling, raised himself up on his elbows and wiped his eyes with his sleeve.

'Lord?' he said, looking around the church. 'Is that you?'

Lilian looked down at the ancient electric heater she had plugged in that morning to take the worst of the cold out of the air. She was resting her freezing feet on it. Could that be what had caused the lights to dim, some loose connection in the wires?

With a quick, guilty glance over her shoulder at the figure of Christ, she shook the heater gently with one foot. The lights dimmed again, twice, as if answering the vicar's question.

He was up on his knees now, a rapt expression on his face. The verger had got out his mobile phone and was filming the whole thing.

'Are you punishing me, Lord? Do you want me to go from here into the wilderness?'

Lilian moved her foot on the heater, and the lights dimmed once. She smiled.

The vicar threw himself back down on the floor and began to sob with relief. Over and over, rattling through the words, he said the Lord's Prayer. Lilian and the verger had to drag him off the floor in the end, and walk him to his car.

By the end of the afternoon, the verger's film had been watched more than 136,000 times online.

The following Sunday, Lilian couldn't believe her eyes when she arrived at the church. The road was blocked, the air filled with noisy car horns as people struggled for parking. The pews were full, as were the extra chairs set out at the end of each pew and most of the aisle. People were reaching up on their toes, better to see.

When the vicar climbed the few steps to the gilded pulpit, an expectant hush fell over the crowd. Lilian reached for the heater with one foot, discreetly.

The vicar, who looked flushed and slightly shaken, opened his Bible. He frowned for a moment as if about to launch into his usual admonishment of those who had dared to turn up, but when he opened his mouth nothing came out. He took his glasses off, closed his eyes and held up both hands.

'Lord, are you there?' he said, looking as though he didn't quite believe himself that God would be.

Lilian shook the heater with her foot and the lights dimmed twice. A sound as of a boiling ocean went through the crowd. Some people began to cry, and man in the aisle fainted and was caught by those nearby. The vicar laughed hysterically.

After ten Sundays on which the church had caused traffic chaos in the neighbourhood, and TV crews from all over the world had been to see God speak to the vicar in what they had dubbed the *Miracle in Dannersgade*, the letter finally arrived from the Ministry of Ecclesiastical Affairs, announcing that Sankt Lukas Kirke had been released from the threat of closure.

Lilian celebrated by staying in the church all night, lighting each and every wax candle she could find, and drinking a bottle of altar wine.

She played Bach till she got cramp in her fingers, then lay down in the aisle and looked up at the ceiling, inhaling the wet smell of ancient stone.

She congratulated herself on her ingenuity. The overcrowded Sunday services and stray parties of tourists who had begun to find their way to the church during the week were a small price to pay for keeping it. Whatever happened from now on, she would never have to leave, except feet first.

Early in the morning, she heard the key turn in the lock. It was Jonas, the handyman, with his box of tools. He had come to fix a tile that had broken and come loose under the weight of the hundreds of new worshippers that attended the church service each week.

Lilian liked Jonas. Unlike most people, he only spoke

when he had something to say. She watched him in silence as he fixed the tile, smoothing the grout with a finger dipped in water, before packing up his tools and getting ready to leave.

'I am glad the church is safe now,' he said on his way out. 'I suppose you could say that God intervened.'

Lilian smiled and nodded. Buoyed by the good night she had had, she decided to test him a little.

'And would you rule out that there could be a logical explanation behind it all?' she said.

Jonas smiled. 'I already thought of that.'

She felt her heart leap into her throat as he gestured at the electric heater by the organ pedals.

'After it happened, the vicar asked me to check every socket and every wire I could find. The plug on that heater of yours was loose, so I changed it, but I found no reason for the lights to dim. I even checked with the electricity board, but nothing out of the ordinary happened on that Sunday, there were no power cuts in any part of the city, and there haven't been any since. It really is a true miracle.'

He smiled, picked up his bag and left.

When the door had clanged shut, and the church was empty and silent, except for the ever-present echoes that were like whispers behind the pillars, Lilian turned her head very slowly to look at the figure of Christ on his crucifix who, for his suffering in death, had always seemed so alive to her. But his eyes were closed, his inscrutable face resting on one shoulder.

Lilian looked up at the east window and wondered for a while how it was possible for the sky to be so blue in February, and the light so extraordinarily bright.

Like White Rain

What angels look like is a matter of opinion. Not to mention whether they exist at all. To Henning, standing ten floors up on the roof of a tower block, the presence of an angel by his side made perfect sense, even a small one in a pink dress. He took the angel to be a messenger from God. Only he did not understand at first what God was saying.

From his position on the ledge it would take him one step to die, a mere flexing of tendons and muscle. Falling into death in this way, by means of a simple command to the brain, had appealed to him before. Now, as his legs refused to budge, he understood that the body will not die so easily.

It was snowing, and the snow was muting the roar of the nearby motorway. In the car park far below, a gang of boys reared their bicycles like hooded horsemen. They did not so much as glance at the woman with the shopping trolley shouting abuse from the street corner opposite. And none of them looked up to see Henning and the angel.

Standing among the satellite dishes and ventilation shafts, Henning observed his world: the familiar streets looked smaller from up there, less significant. He saw the train line running into Copenhagen, the ordered grid of roads like arteries around the heart of the capital.

What is my life for? he asked himself, as he had done so often before. That was when he became aware of a pink flutter by his side. He turned to find the angel looking up at him, a slight, winged figure perched by his side in the fading light.

Fat flakes of snow fell slowly around the two of them as if they were figures inside a snow globe, like the one Henning kept on his sideboard, with the couple kissing on the steps of Notre Dame.

The angel was strangely calm. For a moment Henning considered that he was already dead. He peered over the edge for a glimpse of his corpse slowly spilling its halo of blood across the snow. The angel followed his eyes to see what he was looking at. Then it spoke, and the voice was human.

'Hello.'

Henning saw now that the angel was wearing bright-red lipstick and a plastic wristwatch. Not an angel then, only a girl.

Henning's instinct was to take flight, to hide from

people. But something made him linger. Something he couldn't account for.

'What are you doing?'

Henning thought of the crisp white envelope addressed to his nephew resting against the toaster in his apartment eight floors below. He had planned his suicide carefully and would have resented the girl for spoiling his plans had he not been so relieved.

'Are you going to jump?'

She was winding a strand of her long hair around one finger, fidgeting in the manner of a small child, but her eyes were sincere. Henning shuddered, buried his hands deeper in his heavy overcoat and let his felt hat slip down over his forehead.

'No.'

'What then?'

'I'm just looking.'

'At what?'

'Nothing.'

Henning could not help feeling a certain affinity with the girl. He sensed that she was no stranger to fear, though his was raging with full force, while hers was new.

He decided to leave, but the girl ran after him as he strode towards the stairwell, like a small dog, and, though he didn't want to, he stopped.

'Wait. You're the man next door. What's your name?' she said.

Henning had never seen the girl before. He guessed no one notices a small girl any more than they do an old man.

Her bare arms and legs were mottled purple with cold. She must have been playing in her fairy costume, then dashed up to the roof when she first saw the snow falling outside her bedroom window.

Henning hesitated before answering her, sensing that doing so would be the beginning of something.

'Henning,' he said, finally.

The girl turned her face to the sky for a while, letting the snowflakes melt on her eyelids. Then she said something sad. She said, 'Snow is like white rain. It's just white rain.'

It felt strange to be back in the apartment, having left it a short while earlier for what he thought would be the last time. He left the letter by the toaster, ready for his next attempt. Nothing had changed and nothing would between now and then.

The girl had disturbed him. From his favourite spot in the front room, by the gap in the curtain, he watched her as she came skipping along the walkway outside. She stopped for a moment, so close Henning could have touched her but for the pane of glass. Slowly, she wiped the lipstick off her mouth with the back of her hand. Then she disappeared into the apartment next door.

Why had he never noticed her before? What was her name? How old was she?

Standing in the dark, still in his overcoat, Henning took stock of his failure. If only he had jumped straight away, before the girl had spoken to him, before he knew she was there. If only he had been braver.

Then he remembered what his brain had been trying to tell him. In his mind's eye, he saw the girl again, standing in front of him, covering and uncovering her left arm with her right hand. There was something there on the skin: red marks, ringed with black, like angry eyes.

The girl was the first thing on his mind when he woke up the next morning. He decided it didn't matter if he were to postpone his death for a day.

He went out looking for her, scanning the streets for a flash of pink. He had nearly given up and was walking back towards the block when he saw her. She was on the other side of the street, lagging behind the redheaded woman from next door, and struggling to keep up. She could be no more than eight.

As she passed, she looked straight at him and waved without her mother noticing. No one had ever looked at Henning that way before, as if they could really see him.

He tried but failed to erase the girl from his thoughts. Every day he woke up with a feeling that something exciting was happening. Every day he decided his suicide could wait.

He spent hours standing motionless by the gap in the curtain, watching the girl coming and going. There was a man, too: a skinny, energetic man in a baseball cap and steel-rimmed glasses.

Every evening when going out, the man would stop to light his cigarette outside Henning's window, reappearing in the car park in front of the building a few seconds later. He had a white car, which he drove off furiously, exhaust roaring.

Cigarettes. What had the girl done, Henning wondered, to have them stubbed out on her arm?

One evening after the man had left, and shortly afterwards the woman, there was a knock on Henning's door. It was the girl. Henning felt his heart beat hard in his throat, but he could not resist opening to her.

'Do your mother and father know where you are?"

'Kenneth is not my dad.'

'Who is he, then?'

'Mum's boyfriend. Can I come in?'

'Well, have you told your mother and Kenneth that you're here?'

'They're out. Can I come in?"

'I'm sorry, it's not a good time.'

'Why?'

'I really think you should go home now.'

'Why?'

Henning tried to close the door, but then she did that thing again, covering and uncovering her left arm with her right hand.

'Those marks on your arm. How did you ...?'

The girl looked away, down along the walkway as if hearing someone coming up the stairs, then looked him straight in the eye and said, 'Why were you going to jump?'

It was useless fighting it. Their friendship, however unlikely, had begun. They always met in his apartment. Henning liked to watch her eat: slice after slice of thick white bread, glasses of chocolate milk, apples. The girl liked to look at his snow globe, shaking it vigorously, then pressing her nose against the glass.

One day when she had curled up on his sofa like a cat and fallen asleep, with a small frown pinching the skin above her nose, Henning sat down beside her. He looked at her face, tracing with his eyes the veins that ran like rivers beneath the white parchment of her skin. She stirred, stretched and made herself more comfortable against the cushions and, as she did so, her top slipped a little from her back, revealing an inch of bruised flesh.

Henning gasped, but said nothing about it when she woke up. He and the girl had an unspoken agreement: he did not mention the strange designs on her skin and, in return, she would not bring up his attempt to jump off the roof.

'Are these people your family?' she would say instead, pointing to the photos on his wall.

'Yes, but they are all dead. Well, all except my nephew. He lives in the city.'

'Does he have a nice house?'

'I don't know,' said Henning. 'I have never been invited to his house.'

'Why?'

'I don't know why.'

And so it would go on. The girl would ask the same questions over and over again, and the answers would leave Henning empty.

It was the middle of the night when he first heard the sounds coming from next door. He must have heard them before but blocked them out. The girl's bruises and burns had not made themselves.

The man was shouting drunkenly, and Henning could hear the woman, too, though he could not tell if she was laughing or crying. And then the girl's screams, penetrating the walls and boring into his skull.

He leapt out of bed with an urge to run, to get away, before collapsing in a heap against his front door, pulling the telephone off the hall table.

'Is that the police?'

'Can I have your name?'

'There's a little girl next door, she's screaming. They are hurting her.'

'Your name?'

'I . . .'

'Caller? I need your name and location? Hello?'

He dropped the receiver back in its cradle. He would

be made to sign a statement. They would not understand or believe him. They would ask: How can an old man be friends with a little girl?

He thought someone else would call the police, but the flashing blue lights never came. Then there was silence. Someone slammed the front door. It was him, Kenneth. As always, he lit up before striding off towards the stairs. After a moment, he could be heard driving off.

It happened again, and again.

Somebody had to do something. He wrote to the council, a long letter, setting out the facts as he knew them, but perhaps the letter never reached them, for nothing happened.

The girl grew tired and withdrawn. Several days would pass between her visits, and she became shifty, spending most of her time standing by the window, looking down at the car park and watching out for Kenneth and his white car.

'Mum found out I come in here,' she said to Henning one day. 'She says Kenneth would kill me if he knew – and you.'

Henning hated himself, but he hated Kenneth even more and, in that moment, for the first time, everything made sense: now he knew what God had been trying to tell him on the roof.

The night of the fire it was cold again, cold enough for snow. The booming flash tore an orange strip out of the black sky only moments after Henning watched Kenneth leave the flat next door, stopping briefly to cup his hands around lighter and cigarette. The colours were amazing as the white car went up in flames with Kenneth inside it.

No one notices an old man, any more than they do a little girl. But then Henning had been very careful as he doused the car with petrol, setting it afloat in a rainbow sea. Flicking his cigarette butt out of the window, as was his habit, Kenneth had lit his own funeral pyre.

A few days later, Henning was back on the roof, standing once more on the ledge where death was just a step away. He hadn't seen the girl since it happened. He supposed she was with her mother; it no longer mattered.

He reached into his pocket and pulled out the suicide note addressed to his nephew. He smiled as he imagined his dead sister's son, who never visited him, never phoned and never invited him, not even for Christmas, tearing it open and wondering how much money he had been left.

Then, slowly, Henning ripped the letter. He scattered the pieces and they fell like rain, like white rain onto the people below, who did not notice them and who would never think to look up and see where they were coming from.

The Climbing Rose

Brian riffled through his bag, smiling when he saw the envelope addressed to Mrs Hoffmann. He always made a point of being friendly to the rich old ladies on his round.

He dusted down his red jacket, tucked his hair behind his ears and began to push his bike up the long driveway to the house, whistling as he went.

It had been a while since Mrs Hoffmann last had a proper letter. Usually there were only bills. Brian wondered idly who could have sent it. She had never mentioned any relatives or friends. Sometimes there was post for Mr Hoffmann, but Brian had never seen the man and supposed he must be dead.

Mrs Hoffmann's dog launched into a half-hearted bark up ahead but quickly stopped. Brian guessed it had recognised him by his whistle.

As he got further up the drive, the street noise faded into silence. Klampenborg was like this: big, empty villas surrounded by gardens and hedges reaching up over your head. As soon as you stepped away from the road, you might as well be in another world.

No wonder the old ladies got lonely with no one to talk to for days on end. Brian had only recently started working on this route, but he had soon discovered that he had a talent for listening. He had one of those faces that rich old people trusted.

It was surprisingly easy to gain their confidence. All you had to do was to remember a few things about them: their children's names, their favourite TV programme, the little hobbies they had.

Now and again they would ask him to do things for them. Lift a piece of furniture, change the batteries in the remote control, unscrew the lid from a jam jar. If, afterwards, they slipped him something as a thank you, he couldn't see why that should be anybody's business. It wasn't as if they needed the money where they were going.

Once, one of the old ladies had thrust a 1,000-kroner note into his pocket. Another had given him a pair of gold cufflinks that he had sold on for 1,500. In the past two months, he had almost managed to save enough for a holiday.

Brian stopped to wipe the sweat off his brow. The morning was close and pale, as if a plastic lid had been fitted over

Copenhagen. A humming noise grew out of the silence. Even before Mrs Hoffmann's climbing rose came into view, you could hear them: thousands, perhaps millions, of bees feasting on its sweetness.

The rose was all Mrs Hoffmann ever talked about. She had to be nearly eighty, but she was always out in the front garden, snipping away with her secateurs and carrying watering cans to and fro. He had even caught her mumbling to it a couple of times. You would think it was human, the way she fussed over that thing.

Brian would never say as much to Mrs Hoffmann, but he found the rose a little creepy. There was something unsavoury about its size. The trunk was gnarled and fat, with heavy branches spreading outwards on either side, giving it the look of a giant pair of lungs. With the bees hovering, it seemed almost to be breathing, its flowers gently lifting and falling.

Brian had no idea roses could grow so big. He had once asked Mrs Hoffmann what sort of fertiliser she was using, but she had only tapped her nose and said that a good gardener never gave away her secrets.

The rose had been photographed for the newspapers, apparently, and come first in several gardening competitions. No one had ever seen anything quite like it. Brian reckoned that were it not for the rose, Mrs Hoffmann would lie down and die.

He parked his bike by the front door, trying not to look

up at the house. It was enough to smell the rose. Like old ladies' perfume, its candy sweetness not quite cancelling out the underlying notes of decay. The flowers were vivid in the corner of his vision, as bright red as his uniform, and the size of fists.

In the flower bed by the trunk, Mrs Hoffmann's white terrier was digging frantically, its paws and muzzle soiled. Mrs Hoffmann was bent over next to the dog, her heavy legs sticking out below the old-fashioned housecoat that she always wore for her gardening.

She stood up and smiled at Brian. The climbing rose towered above her, a cascade of red almost completely obscuring the white render of the facade. It could have been his imagination, but Brian thought it had grown at least a few feet since he last saw it. Soon it would climb up over the roof and down the other side.

'Ah, Mr Postman, we have been waiting for you,' said Mrs Hoffmann.

Like most of the old ladies of Klampenborg, she spoke like the Queen, using the second person formal pronoun, which had almost disappeared out of the Danish language.

'You must be telepathic,' he said, putting on his most cheerful voice. 'I have a letter for you. I said to myself, "Mrs Hoffmann is going to be pleased to receive this nice, personal letter."'

She took the envelope from his outstretched hand and, to his astonishment, tucked it away in her pocket without so much as looking at it. Behind her, the dog kept digging, spraying earth in a wide arc onto the lawn.

Brian nodded in its direction, determined not to waste the opportunity at hand. 'I see you are busy. Hot day for it. Say, could I give you a hand with that spade?'

'No need,' said Mrs Hoffmann, her cheeks flushed under her wide-brimmed gardening hat. 'I am almost done. Everything is ready.'

Ready for what? Brian thought. Not for the first time he wondered whether Mrs Hoffmann was a little dotty. A lot of the ladies were. It was all that time spent in their own company.

'But there is another favour I would like to ask you,' said Mrs Hoffmann, wiping a strand of white hair away from her face.

Brian noticed that her hands were covered in scratches, some of them bleeding. 'Of course, I would be glad to help,' he said, placing the bicycle onto its rest.

'You are tall and strong and look like a practical sort of chap. I need a light bulb changing in the kitchen, but the ceiling is too high and even when I stand on a ladder I cannot reach.'

'Sure,' said Brian. 'I can fix that for you in no time.'

He had never been inside Mrs Hoffmann's house before and welcomed the opportunity. In his experience, once you had been invited in and been helpful in one way or another, a handsome tip was sure to follow.

'Good man,' said Mrs Hoffmann.

She quickly mounted the few steps to the front door and led Brian into a dingy hall. The dog didn't look up from its single-minded pawing. A mole, Brian thought, it had caught scent of a mole.

Mrs Hoffmann had absentmindedly brought the spade in with her. Brian noticed for the first time that she had rather strong arms and big hands for her age. He guessed it came from all that gardening.

Inside the house it was impossible to tell whether it was night or day, so little light penetrated through the windows. The branches pressed against the glass, producing an odd squeaking sound. There was a strong smell of damp, and the rooms felt cold, in spite of the heat outside.

Mrs Hoffmann had money all right. Brian noticed several paintings and pieces of porcelain and silver. But the rooms, though expensively furnished, looked as though they hadn't been decorated in decades. Everything was old and worn and had an abandoned look about it.

In the hall there were dozens of framed photographs of Mrs Hoffmann with the climbing rose. In one very old black-and-white photograph, the rose was just knee-high. A man and a woman stood protectively on either side of it, as though it were a child. Brian guessed the man was Mr Hoffmann.

He listened out for creaking floorboards, water running in the pipes, the sound of coughing. Nothing. If he wasn't dead, Mr Hoffmann had to be asleep or out somewhere, which was just fine by Brian. It was always easier when the ladies were alone.

Through the living-room door he caught a glimpse of an armchair by the window. The chair was surrounded by tall stacks of books and magazines and had a reading light directly above it. A teacup and a radio stood on a table to one side. When she wasn't gardening, this was obviously where Mrs Hoffmann passed her time. Perhaps she even slept there, just a pane of glass between herself and her beloved rose.

The kitchen was bare and almost completely dark. In the corners of the windows pale tendrils had pushed their way in, splitting the wooden frame and leaving a trail of paint flakes on the sill. Brian shuddered. Another few years and the rose might have the whole house down.

'Here we are then,' said Mrs Hoffmann, pointing to a ladder directly under the ceiling lamp.

Brian moved towards the ladder, wanting to spin out his good deed for as long as possible. He thought again of the letter that Mrs Hoffmann had tucked away in her pocket.

'Aren't you going to open your letter?' he said.

Mrs Hoffmann shook her head. 'I know what is in it,' she said. 'Now, you should be able to reach from the top step, I think. And here is the new bulb.'

'All right,' he said, taking the light bulb and trying to

think how someone could know what was in a letter without opening it.

A birthday card? An invitation previously discussed over the telephone? In Mrs Hoffmann's case, both seemed unlikely.

The ladder was sturdy enough and when he craned his neck he could see that the old light bulb was still in there. He asked Mrs Hoffmann to check that the lamp was switched off at the socket. Then slowly he stepped up on to the ladder, each step creaking alarmingly under his weight.

When he had reached the top, he unscrewed the old light bulb and rattled it next to his ear, nothing.

Then everything happened very slowly. In a split second, at the same time as he became aware of a shadowy movement behind him, Brian Larsen realised three things: the light bulb didn't need changing; if you wanted the postman to call, the surest way was to post a letter to yourself; and the road had been empty when he had begun to push his bike up the driveway, which meant that no one knew he was here.

And then he was lying on the floor, a loud crashing sound ringing in his ears. The ladder had somehow landed on top of him. He had trouble focusing. When he did, the first thing he saw was his mobile phone. It must have dropped out of his pocket when he fell.

It's all right, he thought. They will be able to trace my phone when I don't come back to the sorting office later.

Then Mrs Hoffmann's spade came down on it, sending glass and metal flying. He guessed that was what she had struck him with. The back of his head felt cold and wet.

He could just about see Mrs Hoffmann's muddy clogs, her sturdy ankles, criss-crossed and bleeding from the thorns.

'I am sorry, Mr Postman,' she said somewhere above him. 'But you see it's for the rose, it's time for her feed. This is not the end, very far from it. You will become part of something extraordinary, possibly the greatest climbing rose there has ever been. People will come from all over the world to see it.'

Brian thought of the dog, its little paws scraping away at the soil and the hole Mrs Hoffmann had been digging when he arrived. Then he thought of the ladder, the way she had set everything up, and he knew that she had done this before.

'Fertiliser,' he mumbled, his mouth rubbery and wet against the tiles, as his vision slowly darkened. 'The gardener's secret.'

The Wailing Girl

Every day, as he started up between the tall, straight lime trees to Brokholm Slot, Magnus Hansen began spontaneously to whistle. Though he would only admit it to himself, the baroque castle, nestled like a cube of sugar in the green and brown fields of North Zealand, induced in him a sense of proprietorship.

Magnus knew every inch of Brokholm, from its hot, dusty attics to its flagstone kitchen floor, worn smooth by generations of servant feet. He was the only one of the visitor guides who could put names to every one of the 378 portraits on the walls. The long-dead aristocrats with their plump faces and naked sideways glances were more familiar to him than his own living relatives.

Magnus disliked members of the public, their rucksacks and grubby hands. No matter how often he told them not

to, they would invariably try to touch things or stray outside the red runners that protected the floors from their
dirty shoes.

Magnus preferred the quiet days when he could wander
Brokholm on his own, seek out an empty wing and step
over the rope partitions to lie in one of the four-poster beds.
Listening to the castle fountains and the peacocks crying
in the woods, he would imagine himself a baron, well-fed
and surrounded by the riches of his seat. Until, invariably,
the present would intrude, announcing itself depressingly
with a scratch from his walkie-talkie as another coachload
of tourists approached from the main road.

Magnus could conduct castle tours in his sleep. He had
a mind for dates and an intimate knowledge of aristocratic
life, eighteenth-century antiques and agricultural imple-
ments. This made it all the more disappointing that visitors
only ever wanted to hear about the wailing girl, allegedly
the ghost of a young maid who was drowned in the moat
by a nobleman after giving birth to his child.

As a guide, he was supposed to mention that, to this day,
the maid could be heard wandering the corridors at night,
crying. But Magnus rarely bothered. He didn't believe in
ghosts, nor had he ever seen or heard one at Brokholm,
wailing or otherwise. Ghosts, in his opinion, were invented
by crafty owners of castles with leaking roofs, mindful that
most people would only pay for history if it came coated in
blood, gore and garishness.

His own business was with the physical world, with bricks and mortar, French clocks, priceless tapestries, oriental screens and marble fireplaces, the way the light slanted like buttermilk through the deep window recesses, pooling on the bowing oak floors.

Magnus did not mix with his colleagues, students mostly, whose tours he considered vastly inferior to his own. He ate his lunch on a bench in the rose garden and pretended to be reading the paper whenever anyone approached.

After work, his black uniform with the red lapels and shiny buttons would smell of Brokholm's sweet, exotic woods, chalky walls and heavy brocades. When Magnus closed his eyes and pressed his nose to the fabric, it was almost as though he were there.

By chance, Magnus had overheard something that he could not stop thinking about. There was a chance, perhaps, that he might one day live at Brokholm as its caretaker.

The castle was presently occupied by Baroness Feltenborg, who kept a small apartment in the east wing, but she was ninety-five and, after her, no one wanted to live there. Magnus guessed that the younger Feltenborgs preferred their modern homes in Copenhagen to the draughty castle. When the baroness died, the estate would pass to a trust, which would have to employ a live-in caretaker, or so Magnus had pieced together. He could see no reason why the caretaker should not be him.

Already he imagined how his life would be. At nights and weekends, he would be free to roam the castle. He had his eye on a costume he had seen on the internet: silk stockings, brogues with silver buckles and a wig. He could light fires and candles, eat his dinner in the banqueting hall and, when night came, take his pick of the twenty-eight beds.

Magnus had never liked old Baroness Feltenborg. Miss Karin, as she insisted on being addressed, had an irritating habit of springing up during his tours. As he and his group of visitors entered a new room, suddenly there she would be, draped on a sofa or standing by a window, a dramatic tableau that made everyone gasp.

In her booming stage-diva voice, Miss Karin, dressed to the nines and leaning dramatically on a stick, would then hold forth on the wailing girl, while the visitors listened with all the rapt attention they had denied to Magnus.

The baroness was sprightly for her age, annoyingly so. Magnus began to fantasise about ways in which she might die: a quick shove down the stairs, a gas leak, a box of poisoned chocolates. Until, little by little, an inspired idea formed in his mind.

It was more difficult than Magnus had thought to recruit an accomplice. After considering a checkout girl in the local supermarket, his hairdresser and a woman who regularly walked her dog past his apartment block, he settled on a young waitress who worked at a café around the corner from his home. From the loud conversations she conducted on her mobile phone, he knew that she was an unemployed actress and struggled for money.

'I have a role for you. It's unusual, but it's acting all the same,' he said to her one day when the café was empty.

At first she was sceptical, but when he had passed her a brown envelope with twenty large notes inside it, she became more attentive.

'Miss Karin, the baroness, is a dear friend of mine and likes a practical joke,' he lied. 'All you have to do is turn up at the castle at one a.m. on Sunday morning. You will find the back door on the latch.'

As for the job itself, he left that to her thespian talent and whatever imagination she could bring to bear on the part. It was best, he explained, if he knew as little as possible about it.

'Is it not illegal?' the waitress asked, but by the way her eyes kept sliding to the brown envelope, Magnus could tell that the money had done its work.

As he left the café, he chuckled to himself, imagining Miss Karin's contorted face, confronted at last with the fictional spectre with which she had entertained legions of visitors to Brokholm.

His plan was to stay away and simply turn up for work on the Monday morning, then watch in sombre shock as the corpse of the baroness was carried out on a stretcher to a waiting ambulance. But as the afternoon sun began to fade over Brokholm on Saturday afternoon, he found himself unable to resist witnessing the performance. He had paid good money for it. Besides, it would allow him to spend his first night at the castle. Seeing as he was going to live there in the future, it was about time.

Magnus raced through the last tour of the day, cutting short his usual script. Afterwards, in front of his colleagues, he made an elaborate show of leaving, getting in his car and driving to the local village, before looping back and parking on a forest track outside the gates.

By the time he walked up the drive, keeping to one side of it in the deep shade of the trees, the sun was setting, the castle a silhouette against the vivid pink sky.

Brokholm felt different at night, each creak and snap of the woodwork amplified in the dark. Magnus had forgotten that he would not be able to switch on the lights. He carried a small torch as part of his uniform, but it was too weak to make much difference, and he could barely see his way around. The immensity of the castle, the weight of its thousands of bricks and beams and roof tiles, seemed to press in on him from all sides.

He had to give himself a stern talking-to: but for the absence of daylight and visitors, the castle was the same as always and thinking otherwise was simply irrational.

He chose a bedroom in the north wing, near enough to Miss Karin's quarters to make up for a front-row seat. It smelt of mildew and cold cinders. He decided against the bed, lest it creaked, instead choosing an armchair facing the door. For a while, he tried to sit in complete darkness, but was disconcerted by the sensation of the eighteenth-century baron Otto Feltenborg staring at him from his full-length portrait on the wall. The only way Magnus could stand it was if he kept the torchlight pointed at the baron's wan face.

It wasn't long before he felt ravenous, as he had not eaten since lunch. For a while he contemplated tiptoeing down to the staff kitchen to look for a biscuit or an apple, but decided it was too risky. Eventually, he fell asleep, drooling on his hand.

It was the wailing that woke him. It had its own rhythm, piercing at first, then unravelling into a series of small sobs. By the direction of the sound, it came from the west wing. Magnus frowned: an interesting choice, to start at the other end of the castle, if a little unnecessary.

He checked his watch. The actress was early – it had only just turned midnight – but that was all right, Miss Karin would have retired a while ago. By now, the ancient baroness would just be opening her eyes, straining to hear the sound that had woken her.

As the crying grew louder, another sound mixed in with it that he could not place at first. Doors, he thought. Doors being opened and shut and urgent running footsteps in between. Of course, the waitress would have done her research: a mother looking desperately for the child that was taken from her by her evil lover, or so the tale went.

She was good, very good, the actress. Though, as the banging and howling neared his room, Magnus thought that perhaps she was going a little too far. Even he was starting to feel uneasy, but he could not very well call out to the actress, unless he wanted to reveal his presence to Miss Karin. Instead, he fumbled with the torch, intending to signal to the girl by way of Morse code that she could skip his room, but the torch would not light. He must have forgotten to switch it off earlier when he fell asleep, and drained the battery.

Too late, he wished that he had stayed at home after all. The girl's wailing really was extraordinarily realistic, not just grief-stricken but furious with it. The kind of fury that could find no release, a roar that was more animal than human.

It occurred to him that he ought to get up, perhaps hide, but all could do was sit there, frozen to his seat and covering his face with his hands like a small boy, thinking this might make him invisible.

The last few running steps outside were agony, though he knew that the actress was only doing what he had asked her to. When finally his door was flung open it was as if from a sudden gust of wind, and not by any hand. In the confusion of the blast and the wailing, he saw nothing but a streak of something grey that looked like moonlight. Then, after what seemed like an eternity, the door was slammed shut and the spectacle moved on, like a terrifying train towards the east wing.

If this was not enough to frighten Miss Karin to death, Magnus didn't know what would be. He almost had been himself and he was the one who had arranged the whole thing.

Soon after, the noise stopped altogether. All the same, Magnus waited several hours before leaving, until the light grew grey at the windows and he was certain the girl had left the castle.

There was nothing on the news about Miss Karin on the Sunday, but then the death of an old baroness from a stroke was hardly the stuff of headlines. It was more disappointing when he arrived for work on the Monday to find no outward sign of disturbance. Despite the drama of Saturday night, it appeared as though nothing had happened.

Later, during a castle tour, Magnus was astonished to come across the baroness herself in the morning room, arranging a bouquet of chrysanthemums to the delight of his gormless charges.

'Tell us, baroness,' he said, exasperated after waiting for her to finish her usual tale about the wailing girl. 'Have you ever heard this ghost yourself?'

'Alas no,' said Miss Karin. A disappointed murmur spread in the room.

The old baroness smiled. 'But then I wouldn't have. You see, I'm stone deaf. Once I remove my hearing aid for the night, you could walk a marching band through this castle and I wouldn't hear it.'

The visitors laughed. Magnus felt his cheeks glow; he had not thought about that. Next time he would have to be a lot more imaginative. Then Miss Karin's face grew serious.

'Which is why there's a problem,' she said. 'Beautiful though it is, none of my descendants are willing to live at Brokholm because of the wailing girl. It won't be easy finding a caretaker willing to stay for more than a few nights.'

Magnus was just about to say that, actually, he'd be happy to oblige if the baroness would do the honours and pass on. That, as a matter of fact, he did not believe a word of all this nonsense about a wailing girl. But at that moment one of his colleagues entered the room.

'There you are. I have been looking for you all morning. A young woman came, told me to give you this.' He passed Magnus a brown envelope.

Magnus stuck his hand inside, finding first the crisp stack of bank notes that he had given to the waitress, then a folded note. The message was extremely brief: *I couldn't do it. Sorry.*

From far off, as his legs buckled under him and the room went dark, he heard the voice of Miss Karin. 'My dear man, are you all right?'

Room Service

Bent had finished most of the bottle and was nodding off in the head chef's chair when the ringing began. He stared at the telephone on the desk in front of him, but the ringing was coming from further away, an old-fashioned sound he had never heard before.

He emerged unsteadily from the cubicle into the gleaming white of the kitchen, scratching his head.

Perhaps it was coming from reception? He knew the night manager had not been able to come in because of the snow.

Whoever it was sounded impatient. As soon as the ringing stopped, it started again.

He went through the corridor with the red carpet gingerly, for the long-dead dignitaries observing him from their frames on the wall made him uncomfortable. He wasn't supposed to stray from the kitchen.

But the ringing was not coming from reception. The light was turned down low, the room deserted and silent.

Bent pressed his forehead against the door to the street, breathing vodka mist onto the window pane and drawing a face with his finger.

The snow was heavy in the cone of street light. There was no sound but the wind. No cars outside, no buses, no people, just a silvery penumbra rimmed by darkness, the buildings across the square as obscure as a distant forest.

It must have been the wind he heard, whistling around the corners of the hotel. That was the trouble with the drink, you couldn't trust your ears, your own eyes. He yawned, scratched the stubble on his scalp, and headed back to the kitchen.

On the radio they were talking about the blizzard as though it were the end of the world. Not since 1978, they said, had the country seen snow like it.

He had just settled back down when the ringing started again. He swore under his breath, switched off the radio and listened hard, hands behind his ears: he heard the water gurgling in the ancient pipes, the humming of the giant fridge, the dripping tap in the pastry section, but still he could not place the sound.

A thought came to him. There was bound to be a telephone in the dining room, though who could be ringing it at this time of night, in this weather?

The room was vast, and the empty chairs seemed to

glare at him disapprovingly, making him nervous. Snow was trickling down the window panes, drawing strange patterns on the walls, the white tablecloths and the arched ceiling with the artificial sky. Blue light twinkled in the chandeliers, the crystal glasses and the silver, as though the entire room were under water. Bent had to lean over for a while, with his elbows resting on his knees.

In the end, he found the telephone in the pantry, next to the dumbwaiter they no longer used. It was an old-fashioned telephone mounted on the wall with a sign above it saying *Penthouse*. It began to ring again, urgently, as he stood there looking at it. Bent did not know the hotel had a penthouse.

Hesitantly, he lifted the receiver. 'Hello?'

The voice on the other end was faint, scratchy and female, barely audible over the yapping dog in the background. It reminded Bent of something, lost in the depths of his memory.

'I wish to place an order, and make it quick.'

'Who is speaking?' Bent said, trying to rein in his drunkenness. 'Listen, if you think you're being funny ...' he began, reckoning it would be someone setting him up for a prank.

Then he remembered the reception was empty and dark. It was two o'clock in the morning. The city was shut down, nothing moving.

He closed his eyes, shook his head to try and sober

himself up, but the voice continued, far away as though speaking down a pipe.

'What, what? Speak up, man.'

Maybe this was something they had forgotten to tell him about in the interview. He hadn't really listened, too desperate to get the job. At his age, with his record, what else was he going to get but the graveyard shift?

Most nights he had very little to do, and free booze, as much as could drink. No one had discovered yet the vodka bottles he had refilled with water and stored at the back of the shelf in the wine cellar.

He fished his pad and pencil out of his pocket.

'What would you like to order, madam?'

'Caviar,' said the woman. 'Lobster Thermidor. Peach Melba. And champagne. Dom Perignon. Iced. For one.'

Bent stared at the pad. At night, in the privacy of their rooms, people ordered burgers and club sandwiches. Filthy food that left them satisfied and ashamed. Lobster Thermidor was not on the menu.

But guests paid a lot of money to stay in the hotel, and he was supposed to cook them whatever they wanted. The head chef had been very specific on that point.

The woman went on. 'Oh, and raw fillet steak, chopped up in the usual manner. Silver bowl.'

She sounded posh and obviously ancient. There was some sort of interference on the line that made it difficult to catch her voice, like dust on an old gramophone record.

He looked helplessly around the kitchen, but, of course, there was no one he could ask. The night waiter had not turned up. He would have to do everything himself.

'Well, man?' said the woman.

'Certainly. Coming right up.'

She said something else after that, something about the snow and the cold, but he couldn't make it out, and then the line cut and she was gone.

He had cooked Thermidor on the cruise ships, a lifetime ago, but cooking was like riding a bicycle, you never forgot how. He whistled to himself as he halved the lobster, removed the meat from the tail and claws and placed it back in the shell. He made the sauce with the butter, shallots and cream, taking a swig from the Cognac and wiping his mouth with his sleeve as he stirred.

On the trolley with the starched white tablecloth he placed the caviar in a silver dish on a bed of ice, surrounded by the unsalted biscuits. Then the grilled lobster and the poached peach in its lake of vanilla ice cream and raspberry sauce. Finally, the silver bowl with the chopped-up sirloin steak, which he took to be for the yapping dog he had heard.

The garish colours of orange, crimson, white and black swam before his eyes, before he topped the plates with the cloches.

He took another swig of the Cognac and checked his reflection in the silverware, squinting at his two faces. His eyes were bloodshot. He rubbed the top of his head with his red, scarred hands and rolled down his sleeves to cover his tattoos. Nothing he could do about the scarlet stain across the front of his whites.

The champagne rattled in its bucket as he pushed the trolley over the uneven tiles. He had never been upstairs to any of the bedrooms before, and was hardly in a fit state now, but what choice was there?

He found the lift to the penthouse around the corner from the new service lifts, an antique contraption with two metal grilles that had to be pulled across and fastened in turn. There was only one button in there. The lift clanged and shook as it travelled slowly past each floor, making the glasses clink. Bent dosed off, waking with a start when the lift shuddered to a halt.

He emerged onto a small landing that led to a corridor with a single door at the end. The Chinoiserie wallpaper and red-shaded lanterns were like something from another time. It took him a long while to find the switch, and even then the light was no more than a faint glow.

There was a fusty smell and something else, cloying and mossy, like bath salts. Violets, he thought, just like candied violets.

The door looked tiny and seemed to get further and further away as he made his way down the corridor, pushing the rattling trolley ahead of him.

He noticed the door was ajar, the smell of violets stronger

than before. He knocked, trying to glimpse something, anything, beyond the darkness.

'Hello? Room service.'

He knocked again, harder. Most likely she was deaf as a post.

'Room service!'

Nothing. Perhaps she meant for him to come in and that was why she had left the door open. He stepped in cautiously, wary of the yapping dog. But there was no sign of the creature, nor of the mad woman, just the scent of violets.

The room was not entirely dark, he saw now. Beyond the bulky contours of the furniture was a large window overlooking the square and the rooftops, the odd street light glimpsed through the snow like a star through thin cloud. He had never see the city like this before, laid out below him, white, clean, frozen.

There was an armchair there, in front of the window, and beside it a table. He drew a finger across the surface; it came back fuzzy with dust.

'Hello?' his voice echoed in the empty room.

He found two doors, one to a bathroom and one to what he assumed was a bedroom, but no one answered his call, and the rooms were draughty and damp.

The call he had taken in the kitchen seemed like something that had happened a long time ago. There was nothing here, nothing but the scent of violets that came and went and came again.

What was it about violets, the way they robbed you momentarily of your senses?

Suddenly he was afraid.

He ran a bit with the trolley, making a mess of the caviar and crackers and knocking over the champagne flute. It was as though the lift would never come, then an eternity before it reached the kitchen, clattering through every storey. This time he was awake, his eyes wide in the mirror on the panelled wall. The iodine waft of caviar and raw steak was noxious in the small space.

He sat for a while in the kitchen and looked at the trolley, willing his heart to slow down. He sat there staring until the lobster was stone cold and the ice cream melting. As he looked on, one of the crackers dropped from the silver dish and split in two, the caviar staining the white tablecloth purple.

He corked the champagne into his fist and drank it straight from the bottle. In time, he fell asleep, his chin resting on his chest, his legs splayed on the cold tiles.

It was the head chef himself who woke him, shaking him roughly by the arm. 'What do you think you're doing?'

There was a lot of noise in the room, the clanging of pots, people shouting across at one another. The light was too bright. He squinted, a hand over his eyes.

'There was an order last night,' he mumbled, his mouth like glue. 'From the penthouse. But no one was there, no one at all.'

Someone near him laughed.

'What in God's name are you talking about? The penthouse hasn't been used for years, not since the roof caved in.'

The head chef kicked the champagne bottle, sending it rolling across the floor.

'Go home Bent, you're drunk. This will be coming out of your wages.'

They wouldn't listen. They laughed at him when he showed them the old phone, the pad with the order written in his snarled, drunken hand in the dead of the night.

He got to his feet and stumbled towards the door. He was almost at the staff exit when he turned around.

They weren't supposed to go through the corridor with the pictures. Not with guests around, not in the daytime. But there it was, the portrait of the woman with the stern expression and the long nose, and the little white dog, cradled in her jewelled hand.

Elizabeth Amalie Rosendahl. Founder.
Died in the Great Winter Storm of 1978.

He ran straight out of the front entrance into the glassy darkness of the street, where the snow had turned slushy, and the cars and people had returned as though nothing had happened.

He bumped into a woman carrying luggage. The bags

tumbled noisily on the pavement, and the doorman shouted at him, but it wasn't till he had reached the other side of the square that something made him turn, and he could have sworn that he saw a light in the window set high up in the roof of the hotel, briefly, like the flicker of an eye.

This time Bent kept running as fast as he could, barely noticing the people who stopped to stare at the bald man in the check trousers and whites, with the scarlet stain down his chest, skidding across the snow in his clogs and looking as though he had seen a ghost.

The Ghost of Helene Jørgensen

Øresund had never been so still, so perfectly flat: a giant silver dish rimmed by a thousand lights twinkling along the Swedish coast. Cecilie cooled her forehead against the window of her office. It was as close to day outside as it is possible for a moonlit winter night to be. Blue and bright and strange, as though the Star of Bethlehem itself had descended on Copenhagen.

There was a knock on the door. She frowned. The latest admission had been strapped down and sedated earlier in the evening, but the nurses were under strict instructions to fetch her whenever she was needed, no matter how late. She replaced her spectacles, smoothed down her silk shirt and brushed a strand of hair from her forehead.

'Enter.'

A male face appeared in the door. The face was wide

and fleshy, the nose big with flayed nostrils from which sprouted several black hairs

'Oh,' the man said.

'Looking for a patient?' Cecilie asked.

Occasionally someone would visit a parent or spouse on the major holidays. She assumed that the man had taken a wrong turn and got himself lost, but he shook his head.

'Actually, I was after Doctor Lindegaard.'

'You're looking at her.' She waited patiently for his surprise to pass.

The man's eyes were bloodshot, his cheeks red. There was a raw patch above one ear with evidence of repeated scratching.

'You're really a doctor?' he asked.

She let it go. 'I'm the resident psychiatrist here. And you are?' she asked.

The man cast his eyes back out to the corridor, looking left and right, then entered her office and closed the door behind him. Cecilie felt for the panic button in her trouser pocket. The security guard was only fifteen seconds away, if it came to it.

'They let me in. Told them I had an appointment,' the man said, holding upon his hands in a gesture of apology. 'I found your name on the internet.'

'An appointment? On Christmas Eve?' Cecilie said.

'Told them it was an emergency,' the man said. 'Which is true.'

He glanced quickly around her office, seeming to find reassurance in her white coat and stethoscope hanging from a peg behind the door, and, at the other end of the room, the couch with the clean paper napkin spread across the headrest.

'I'm here about me,' he said. 'I need your help urgently.'

The door to Cecilie's private apartment was ajar, the edge of her bed just visible across the hallway. She closed the door quickly before the man had a chance to look. Then she sat down behind her desk with the view of the sound, switched on the yellow-glowing desk lamp, and pointed to the chair opposite.

'Take a seat for a moment, Mr ... ?'

'Jørgensen.' The man sat down, but almost immediately jumped up again and stared wildly at the door. 'Who's that?'

Then Cecilie heard it, too, the echo of approaching footsteps, clogs on concrete, a faint jingle of keys. The security guard, tall and bearded, stuck his head around the door and glanced threateningly at the visitor.

'Everything all right here, Doctor Lindegaard?'

Cecilie looked at Jørgensen, who was smiling disarmingly. She nodded. 'I believe so.'

'He insisted he had an appointment,' said the guard.

'Really, it's fine,' Cecilie said. 'You can go back to your desk now.'

The guard looked unconvinced.

'I take it the nurses have brought you down some Christmas dinner?' she asked, to appease him.

The guard smiled broadly. 'I was just about to tuck into it. We're all meeting up in the staffroom later to light the tree. Won't you be joining us?'

Cecilie thought longingly of the expensive bottle of Burgundy waiting in her apartment. She shook her head, smiled and patted the pile of papers on her desk.

'Too much work to do, I'm afraid.'

'Well, goodnight then,' the guard said, pausing on the threshold to throw Jørgensen one last menacing look.

When he had left, Cecilie turned to her visitor.

'The staff here are very protective of me.'

'I can see that,' said Jørgensen. 'And very wise too, with all those mad people about. A dangerous place for a woman to work, I would have thought.'

Cecilie felt her shoulders tensing but twisted her mouth into a smile. 'On the contrary, I prefer it. Life is very predictable in here, safe.'

'Are you saying you prefer lunatics to normal people?' said Jørgensen.

'It can often be hard to tell the difference,' said Cecilie under her breath.

She looked down at her scarred hands and moved them out of sight under the desk. 'You must understand, Mr Jørgensen, that this is an asylum, a hospital for the mentally ill, not a walk-in medical practice.'

'I know,' he said, undeterred. 'And that's exactly why I am here. I think I am losing my mind. I need ... something, to sleep, to calm me down.'

His eyes searched the shelves behind the desk. 'You keep medicine here, don't you? I can pay,' he said, patting his pocket.

'Now look here—' Cecilie cut herself off, distracted.

A tall, elegant woman had appeared outside. She was standing motionless in the moonlight, staring intently through the window. The light reflected metallically off her black fur coat and fur hat, and her face was as white as porcelain, the lower half lost in shadows.

'Your wife ... is she with you?' Cecilie began, gesturing over Jørgensen's shoulder at the window, but he had buried his face in his hands.

'Oh, my wife. My poor wife,' he said, scratching furiously at the red patch above his ear. 'I don't know what to do.'

'Very well,' Cecilie said, checking her watch. 'I guess I can spare a few minutes, but as a state employee I can't accept any form of payment.'

Jørgensen thought about this briefly, then nodded in agreement. He reached into the pocket of his coat. 'Do you mind?' he said, sucking hard on an electronic cigarette. 'I find it calming.'

'Go ahead.'

She dismissed an urge to fetch her own out of the desk drawer, afraid of the familiarity it might suggest.

Soon, clouds of vapour swirled above Jørgensen's head. He loosened his collar and patted his brow with a dirty handkerchief.

Carefully considering how to begin, Cecilie glanced over the man's shoulder at the woman outside. She had not moved an inch. Her eyes were piercing, dark hollows, making Cecilie shudder.

Jørgensen did not turn to look. His hand was shaking badly. Cecilie shifted in her seat, reached for her pad and pen.

'You're married, you said.'

He nodded miserably.

'And what do you do?' she probed.

'My father was a builder. We didn't have much; I left school early. But a few years back, I got a job in a furrier's just around the corner from the Royal Theatre.'

Cecilie knew the place, recalled a large black sign with elegant gold lettering above the door, a line of trees along the pavement.

'I am familiar with it,' she said.

'Well, that's where I met Helene. She was the owner's daughter and a few years older than me, used to come and help out in the shop now and again. We married, and when her old man passed away we took over the shop.'

'And now?'

'In the past few weeks I have not been able to open for business, though Christmas is our busiest season. God help me, I can't sleep at night, and during the day I cannot keep my eyes open. It's the only time when I can get a little rest from it.'

'From what, Mr Jørgensen? What's keeping you awake at night?'

'The voices – I'm hearing voices. That means I'm going mad, doesn't it? Go on, say it!'

'Don't upset yourself. Just answer my questions, if you would. Tell me about the voices you've been hearing,' Cecilie said.

'It's her, Helene,' he shouted. 'Clear as day. Sometimes whispering, sometimes shouting. There is never a moment's pause.'

Cecilie lifted her glasses and rubbed the bridge of her nose.

'Your wife talks to you all night?' she said wearily. 'May I suggest you sleep in another room? Or ask her to be quiet?'

Jørgensen stood up, placed his large hands on the desk. 'You don't understand!' he shouted. 'Helene ... she's dead.'

'She is?' Cecilie was confused. She glanced at the woman in the fur coat, who was still standing stock-still outside the window. 'When I asked earlier if you were married, you confirmed it. You left me to think—'

'But I *am* married,' he insisted. 'Kristina, God bless her sweet heart, is my second wife. We married in October.'

'I see.' She picked up the pad and pencil again, made a few notes. 'Please do sit down, Mr Jørgensen. Try to stay calm. Your first wife, was she ill?'

'No,' he said, as though he wished it had been so. He buried his face in his hands again, groaning loudly.

'She drowned, out there on the sound. We own a yacht; it used to be her father's. One Sunday on our way back to the marina my wife fell overboard in rough weather. I tried to rescue her, but she was lost.'

His level tone of voice suggested he had recounted the events many times before.

'I am sorry,' Cecilie said.

Jørgensen shrugged unhappily.

'Sometimes,' he said. 'I feel as if she is there in the room, or behind me in the street, taunting me.'

'And what does she say?'

'She says ...' Jørgensen swallowed and stopped. Cecilie urged him with her eyes to go on.

'She says I killed her and stole her father's money.' He pressed his hands to the side of his head and moaned. 'She haunts me, even from the grave. Look at me – I am a wreck.'

'And did you?' Cecilie said, a bit more sharply than she intended.

Jørgensen looked dazed. 'Pardon?'

'Do those things she said?'

'Absolutely not. It was an accident. The money became

mine on her death, fair and square. My wife was an only child, see?'

Jørgensen held Cecilie's gaze with his bloodshot eyes till she had to look away. Now she noticed his hands. His suit was expensive, his coat had a mink collar, but his hands were large and rough, like those of a labourer. They trembled slightly.

'Was your first marriage a happy one?' she asked, a twitch of anxiety in her abdomen.

Jørgensen appeared put out. 'We had our ups and downs, same as everybody else.' He paused, glared at her.

'Are you married, Doctor Lindegaard? Because then you will know exactly what I mean.'

'I used to be,' Cecilie said, nodding. *Ups and downs* was hardly an adequate term for Morten's violent temper, she thought.

Jørgensen leant back smugly, as though she had just proved his point. 'Well then.'

She raised her voice, her cheeks tingling with indignation: 'People might say you remarried rather quickly after your first wife's death. Tell me, were you and this Kristina seeing each other before the boating tragedy?'

Jørgensen's smile vanished. 'What are you getting at?'

'Does that mean yes?'

He stared at her defiantly. 'She worked in the shop. I don't believe it's illegal to marry a member of one's staff.'

He jumped out of his seat. 'Actually,' he said. 'I think I

have told you more than enough. Now will you give me something?'

When she did not react, he folded his hands in mock prayer. 'Please, doctor. If it doesn't stop, I will lose the shop. Kristina will leave me, I will have nothing left.'

Cecilie looked out at the woman who kept staring in through the window. Her eyes were fixed on Jørgensen's back. Behind her were the silvery waters of the sound and, further along the coast, the slumbering heart of the city. How long since Cecilie had been to Copenhagen, or even outside the asylum? Last she heard, Morten was still working at the same hospital, but he wouldn't come after her now, not after so many years. Would he?

'There are certain drugs,' she said, caressing the silky ridges on her hands under the table. 'Relaxants, sleeping pills, that sort of thing. But they will not cure the underlying cause of your condition. Someone would need to diagnose you properly.'

She wasn't prepared for Jørgensen's reaction. With an astonishing agility for someone so heavy, he leant across the desk and grabbed her by the collar of her shirt before she could press the panic button. Limply, she reached out for the desk phone, but it was too far away.

'You think you're so clever,' he shouted. 'Sitting here in your cosy office and passing judgement. You don't know what it's like to lie awake all night, to constantly look over your shoulder to see who is there, to never be at peace.'

'Oh, but I *do* know. I know exactly,' Cecilie said, managing to speak in a level tone of voice and looking Jørgensen in the eye, though her body had become liquid with fear.

'Is this the way you treated your first wife, Mr Jørgensen?' she said.

They stood like that for a while, struggling, their grotesque amalgamated form reflected in the windowpane. Her hands had reared up, a long-remembered gesture of protection. Morten had liked to come at her with his belt, the buckle splitting her skin open across the backs of her hands.

The woman outside had not moved. She was still staring at Jørgensen, transfixed, unblinking. In the frozen, still air, she appeared to be floating.

Cecilie pointed over Jørgensen's shoulder. 'Your wife, why is she out there in the cold? And why does she keep standing there, staring at you like that?'

Jørgensen let go of her shirt and turned wide-eyed towards the window. Then he began to splutter. He clutched at his chest with both hands, shoulders hunched, his face crimson.

'Her ... she is dead, dead,' he rasped, pointing at the window, before collapsing on the rug.

Cecilie knelt down and felt for his pulse. His heart had stopped. She spent some minutes in a vain attempt to resuscitate him, but Jørgensen was gone. When she looked up at the window again, the woman had vanished, as if she had never been there in the first place.

Cecilie ran down the corridor, almost colliding with the security guard coming the other way on his regular rounds. 'Did you see her?' she shouted. 'The woman outside my window?'

'Who?' The guard had dribbled gravy down the front of his white shirt. 'I have not seen a soul all evening besides your visitor, and all the wards are quiet,' he said. 'What is it, Doctor Lindegaard? What's happened? You look white as a sheet.'

She didn't stop to explain. 'The man you let in,' she shouted. 'He is dead, in my office. Call an ambulance and the police. Tell them there is no rush.'

Without looking back, she ran down the drive, away from the asylum, her footsteps curiously light and silent on the snowy ground. She trembled, her hands fluttering like white birds against her body.

The woman was halfway down the road outside the gates by the time Cecilie caught up with her. She was almost as tall as the square dark hedges that lined the pavement, buffering the neighbourhood's large villas from public view. Her breath hung in a white cloud about her fur hat.

'Stop,' Cecilie shouted after her. 'Who are you?'

The woman stood very still for a moment with her neck bent. Then she turned and removed her hat, a dowdy middle-aged woman with a defeated look in her eyes.

'I think you must have worked that out by now,' she said.

In the silence, from one of the nearby houses, came the faint sound of singing, a Christmas hymn. Cecilie recognised the words: 'Heart, lift thy wings of joy.'

'Is he dead?' Helene Jørgensen asked, finally.

'Yes. Nothing I could do.'

'Good,' said Helene. She sighed. 'Then I expect you will want to report me to the police.'

'Should I?' Cecilie asked.

'He married me for my father's money, and I took him because no one else wanted me. Then he pushed me into the sea,' Helene said.

'But you survived.'

'A Swedish boat picked me up. I was barely alive.' She smiled sadly. 'I watched my own funeral from behind a tree. He kissed that girl by my graveside.'

'Kristina.'

She closed her eyes, whispered 'Yes.' She shook her head as if to rid herself of the memory. 'Well, you saw tonight what kind of man he is.'

'What did you do?' Cecilie said. 'I mean afterwards?'

'I stayed in Sweden for a while. The police would have been very interested in hearing from me. My husband might have been in jail by now, but I wanted him to suffer. So I started letting myself in to our apartment and hiding in cupboards, behind the curtains or under the table.'

'And you spoke to him.'

'Yes.'

They stood like that for a while. Cecilie was the first to break the silence. 'Assuming I *don't* tell the police about you, what will you do now? Where will you go?'

The tall woman shrugged. 'Helene Jørgensen is dead. That makes me a ghost, and ghosts are free to go wherever they want.' She lowered her voice. 'If you will let me?'

Cecilie nodded slowly.

They shook hands and a look passed between them. Then Helene Jørgensen turned and walked down the road, towards the water in which she was given up for dead, her footsteps hushed by the snow.

When she had gone, Cecilie started walking back towards the asylum. Jørgensen's death would have to be explained. There would be forms to fill in, statements to be made. They would have to tighten security and she would be reprimanded for not raising the alarm sooner.

She sighed, then stopped walking, hesitated.

After a few minutes, an ambulance, closely followed by a police car, came creeping quietly up the road, their blinking lights flickering across the iron railings.

Cecilie made a swift decision and pressed herself against a laurel hedge, making herself one with the foliage. The drivers did not see her.

If not for her white, steamy breath or the long black shadow she cast in the snow, she could have believed herself invisible then.

She did not feel cold at all, but drunk on the sharp, new air, on the sight of the road down which the ghost of Helene Jørgensen had so effortlessly vanished.

Before she knew it, Cecilie was running, lighter and faster with each step, away from the asylum, towards the train station and the city and the strange blue night.

The Suitcase

At Kastrup Airport, it was late but still light, as though a layer of blue gauze had been draped over Copenhagen. Had Hopkins not dawdled in that curious midsummer night, causing him to end up behind a flight from Alicante in the passport queue, it would not have happened.

When he reached arrivals, the baggage carousel was empty. Before he had even opened his mouth, the blonde woman behind the desk passed him a card with pictures of suitcases. He pointed to one that looked like his. Black, medium-sized, retractable handle, wheels.

The woman pushed a form across the desk for him to fill in. 'We'll contact you if it turns up.'

'If?' he said, and the woman shrugged.

Hopkins made a quick inventory. The suitcase held his clothes, his order forms and the list of clients he was supposed to visit in the next five days. A spasm seized his throat at the thought of it. As he walked out through customs, empty-handed, he had to steady himself on a wall.

At the hotel, he sat on his bed without removing his coat and looked out the window. He thought, I am in a city I don't know, with nothing but the clothes I am wearing.

The hotel was opposite Tivoli Gardens. The amusement park was shimmering with lights. He could hear the screams – the mechanical grind of the rides that rose high above the trees. People with their legs dangling free were being hoisted up the side of a tall, golden tower then sent tumbling to the ground. Hopkins had to look away.

His mobile phone rang, number unknown. Perhaps it was the woman at the airport. Perhaps they had found his suitcase already.

'Mr Hopkins?' The voice was male, old and heavily accented.

'Who is this?'

'You don't know me, but I'm afraid I have your suitcase. I took it, at the airport.'

'Thank God,' Hopkins said. The man must have found his number on the name tag. 'Are you still at the airport?'

'No.'

'In that case, you can bring it to my hotel. I am in the centre, opposite Tivoli.'

'I don't walk so well. Could I possibly ask you to come here instead? It will be the quickest way.'

Hopkins thought for a moment. Could it be a scam? He had never heard of such a thing.

'I suppose so,' he said.

'Very good. I'll send a car for you. When you get here, go to the fourth floor.'

There was a click. The man was gone before Hopkins could ask why the suitcase could not simply be sent along.

The car turned out to be an old but well-kept black Mercedes. Hopkins hesitated on the kerb, unsure whether to wait for the uniformed driver to get out and open the door. After a few minutes in which nothing happened, he let himself in and sat on the back seat.

As they set off, the doors locked with a snap. There was a pane of tinted glass between himself and the driver.

What am I doing, getting into a car with a stranger in a city I have never been to before? Hopkins thought, his palms tingling.

He tried to memorise the journey, but soon had to give up. They drove past endless blocks of lit-up apartment blocks down boulevards, along dark lakes bordered by trees. He was almost certain they passed the same square twice. Finally, the driver pulled up outside an imposing, neoclassical building. It was a good few minutes before Hopkins realised he was meant to get out.

The door to the building was ajar. As Hopkins walked

towards it, the Mercedes sped away and disappeared around the corner.

There was a lift. It had a polished wooden door with a porthole window. It was slow and very small, and made a loud knocking sound as it passed each floor.

The landing had elaborate balustrades and was lit by crystal lights set into grey and white panelling. There was only one door. Hopkins rang the bell and, after a while, heard a soft shuffle inside.

The door was opened slowly, revealing a well-dressed elderly man with thick horn-rimmed glasses and a face riddled with liver spots. He was leaning on a walking stick. A faint smell of cigar smoke emanated from the apartment, and somewhere inside there was music playing, a soft piano.

'Ah,' the man said. 'Mr Hopkins. I trust the drive was all right?'

Hopkins immediately relaxed. His suitcase was standing right there in the hallway.

'Yes, thank you. Though your driver doesn't say very much.'

The old man smiled. 'Otto is ... how do you say it ... a man of few words. Please, do come in.'

Hopkins glanced at the suitcase, but decided it would be impolite not to spare a couple of minutes.

They walked through to a spacious, elegantly furnished living room in which three walls were taken up entirely by shelves crammed with books, pictures and artefacts. A half-smoked cigar was smouldering in an ashtray by a winged armchair.

When Hopkins had taken it all in, his gaze fell again on the old man, who was staring up at him with bemused interest.

'I'm sorry,' Hopkins said. 'But I don't believe I saw you on my flight.'

'Oh, but I wasn't.'

'No? So where *did* you come from?'

'Does it matter?' the old man said, still smiling. 'I arrived. I went through baggage reclaim. I picked up a suitcase.'

Hopkins shook his head. 'You are supposed to go to the baggage area that's allocated to your flight. That's where your suitcase will be,' he explained patiently.

'You misunderstand,' said the old man. 'Whenever I arrive home at Kastrup, I pick up a suitcase. It is always most exciting to see what I get.'

'You can't just take any old suitcase.'

'Why not? They are right there, on the conveyer belt, freely available. A smörgåsbord, if you like.'

Hopkins found it hard to maintain an even tone. 'It's theft.'

The old man waved his hand dismissively. 'Ownership is transient, Mr Hopkins. None of us are here for long. And when something is lost, it is an opportunity for something new to be found in its place, don't you think?'

He leaned in close, revealing rather yellow teeth and a breath smelling of brandy. 'They lose millions of suitcases in airports. It's not as if anyone is going to notice, is it?'

Hopkins stared at the old man.

'Wait just a minute,' he said. 'If that's the way you see it, why did you call me?'

'To tell you the truth, Mr Hopkins, I took pity on you.'

Hopkins stepped away, shaking his head in disbelief. 'Look here. Whoever you are, you are obviously mad, and you are breaking the law. I would like to have my suitcase, now.'

'Of course. And Otto here would be delighted to take you back to your hotel.'

Hopkins spun around. The driver had entered the room soundlessly. Standing up, he was surprisingly big. His eyes, deep-set in folds of pale flesh, were fixed on Hopkins.

'Look,' Hopkins said, holding up both hands and forcing his voice down into a lower register. 'I meant no offence. Let me just take my things and be out of here.'

He returned to the hall, followed closely by the old man and his driver. The suitcase was still there, but he now saw that the address label was missing. He knelt down, unzipped the lid and peered inside. The first item he saw was pink. 'This isn't my luggage,' he exclaimed.

'I never pretended it was,' said the old man. 'I thought you might have more fun with this one.'

'Where is my suitcase? What have you done with it?' Hopkins shouted.

He noticed a long corridor leading from the entrance hall. Seeing what he meant to do, the driver advanced quickly to stop him, but the old man held up his hand.

'It's quite all right, Otto. Let Mr Hopkins see for himself.'

There were a number of doors. Hopkins tried the first. He let out a small gasp. The room was full of suitcases, dozens of them stacked up to the ceiling. All of them black, medium-sized with retractable handles and wheels.

He tried the next room and the two rooms after that. All of them were full of suitcases, varying only slightly in size and style. A paper label had been attached to each with a place name and a date written in blue ink. *Morocco, 16 April, 2003. Berlin, 5 December, 1992. Rio de Janeiro, 22 February, 1996.*

'Come,' said the old man, leading Hopkins through to the last room, in which the suitcases were noticeably older. He reached up and pulled one down from the top of a pile, releasing a fine shower of dust.

'My first. Venice, fifth of July, 1976. I took this one by mistake.'

He opened it carefully, flicking open the brass latches on either side of the handle. A smell of mildew rose from the contents. 'Look at all this,' he said. 'Exquisite jewellery, books of poetry, dresses, underwear of purest silk. You can see the owner before you, can you not? A life, neatly stowed inside a box.'

He closed the suitcase, affectionately brushed the dust

from its lid. 'I made my money collecting antiques all over the world. After that day, I started on suitcases, too. You won't find a collection quite like this one.'

Hopkins opened and closed his mouth. There had to be more than a thousand suitcases in the apartment. 'Where is mine? Where have you put it?' he asked in a voice that had scarcely any force to it.

'Ah, yours,' replied the old man, leaning on his walking stick with Otto blocking the light in the doorway behind him.

'Yours was, shall we say ... a little disappointing. I thought to myself, Who travels with five identical white shirts and five identical grey ties? Who rolls his socks and irons his undergarments? Tell me, Mr Hopkins. Have you ever considered wearing different colours, something a little brighter, perhaps? I think it would suit you.'

Hopkins felt close to tears. 'I just want my suitcase back. I beg of you, tell me where it is.'

He wanted to turn back the clock and come out of the plane again and this time go straight to arrivals and pick up his suitcase and go to his hotel and go to bed.

'I have appointments,' he said. 'People are expecting me in the morning. I can't just ... there are things I have to do.'

'Very well,' said the old man, snapping his fingers at Otto. 'Get Mr Hopkins his luggage. He is quite sure he wants it back.'

The driver returned with the suitcase. Hopkins zipped it open. It was his. Everything was in place.

'Thank you,' he said, hanging his head.

'Otto, Mr Hopkins is tired. Take him to his hotel,' the old man said.

In the lift, the driver's button eyes were blank, as though nothing out of the ordinary had happened.

Fifteen minutes later, Hopkins was back in his room. Though it was past midnight, it was still not completely dark. Exhausted, he undressed, tumbled straight into bed and fell asleep immediately with one hand on the suitcase safely ensconced on the floor beside him.

In the morning, he lay in bed, staring at the ceiling and thinking about the apartment with the luggage lost forever to its owners. When he couldn't delay any longer, he got up and opened the suitcase.

He rubbed his eyes. It wasn't his. It was the other suitcase, the one from the old man's entrance hall. Uppermost inside was a pink shirt and, beneath it, a purple tie with bright flowers and a cream linen suit.

Hopkins glanced at his own clothes, tossed in a grey heap on the floor. Then he stood in front of the full-length mirror and held up the stranger's shirt. It smelt faintly of cologne.

Through the open window came the sounds of the unfamiliar city stirring into life. Soon the rides would start up again, the screaming that was half terror, half pleasure. It would take just a few minutes to stroll across the street, pick up a ticket and walk through the turnstile.

Hopkins cocked his head and ran a hand through his hair, looking himself up and down. As he pulled on the pink shirt, slowly fastening each of its pearl buttons, his heart began to beat very fast.

The Tallboy

He saw the woman coming: her wide eyes as she leant over the passenger seat and looked up at the sign above his shop, the large object under the blanket in the back of her Volvo, the expensive handbag in the crook of her elbow as she opened the door. He saw all this from behind his desk and he knew he had something good.

'It says in the phone book that you buy antique furniture – any antique furniture?'

She bit her lip, leaving a smear of lipstick on her front teeth.

'You have been correctly informed, best prices you will find anywhere in Copenhagen,' he said, smiling but not getting up from his chair. Not yet.

She came closer, her gaze gliding over the wardrobes, dressers and commodes jostling for space in the narrow room, before settling on the mug of coffee and half-finished crossword on his desk. Her nose wrinkled at the smell of the turpentine and linseed oil coming through the open door to the workshop at the back. He became conscious of his calloused hands, the dark half-moons under his nails.

'I wonder if you could take a look at something for me,' she said. 'It's outside, in the back of my car.'

'What is it?' he said, still not getting up. No need to seem keen.

'Just an old chest of drawers.'

As she led him out of the shop, jangling her car keys, he tried not to walk too fast. He could smell her perfume, see the dark roots where her blonde hair parted. She had laid down the back seat of her car to make room for the chest. The size and shape of it gave him a good feeling. When you had been in the business for as long as he had, you developed a nose for these things.

When she pulled back the blanket, his breath caught in his throat. It was a tallboy the colour of plump chestnuts, luminous in the winter gloom. He winced on seeing how roughly she had handled it. Flame mahogany, most likely Cuban, cut from the underarm of the tree, shipped to Europe and fussed over for months by long-dead cabinetmakers in London, and she had thrown it into the back of her car with nothing but a stained dog blanket for padding.

'It was my father's. We have had to put him into a home, so ...'

She trailed off and half smiled at him. He noticed that there were dark rings under her eyes and, despite himself, felt a flare-up of sympathy. Though it was now some years in the past, he remembered that his own mother's illness and eventual death had been a strain. But then again, what did he have in common with this rich woman from the suburbs? He imagined her big villa, the sleek white walls, the designer furniture. How she would have gone through her father's things, dismissing them as worthless junk, chucking the tallboy in her car to get rid of it. They had no idea, these people, no idea at all.

'I don't know,' he said, stroking his chin. 'I would need to get it out into the light to have a proper look.'

It always worked, especially with the larger items. Get them into the shop and people were much less likely to want to take them away again, even if the money was less than they were expecting.

They worked together on his instructions, carrying first the bottom half into the shop, then the top, carefully slotting it into place. There was a difficult moment when the woman, who seemed to be half in a daze, nearly dropped one of the drawers on the pavement and he couldn't stop himself from crying out, but she took no notice. Soon they had the tallboy assembled.

'Well?' she said.

You only had so much luck in life. Once, he had found a diamond necklace at the back of a wardrobe that he had picked up for nothing in a house auction. Another time, a French chair had turned out to be sixteenth-century walnut and extremely rare. The tallboy was better than that.

It was English, almost certainly mid-eighteenth century. The drawers smelled of cigar boxes and brought to his mind images of the ancient tropical forests of Latin America. She watched as he pulled gently to release the secretaire behind the two fake drawers in the middle, revealing the most extraordinary example of rosewood veneer-work he had ever seen. His heart was beating so hard he thought it must be visible to the woman.

He took his time, running his hands up and down the sides of the chest, as smooth and dense as marble. He tapped the back, opened each of the little drawers in the secretaire and leant down with a magnifying glass to inspect the intricate inlaid motif on the centre panel, some sort of gargoyle or demon. He noticed that the panel was badly dented and scratched around the edge, but nothing that a little loving care in his workshop wouldn't put right.

'Yes, it's as I thought,' he said, pointing at random to one of the drawers. 'Do you see that colour difference? This entire panel is reproduction. I expect it was added some-time in the 1960s.'

'I see,' the woman said.

'You used to get good prices for these, but now, well, the trouble is that there are so many of them on the market, so unless they are in prime condition ...'

He ran his finger over the dented panel.

'Hmm,' she said. 'Yes, I see.'

He had prepared himself to qualify his response in some way, to answer probing questions, but the woman said nothing more, merely shifted her weight from one foot to the other and looked up at him expectantly.

'Tell you what,' he said, finally. 'Seeing as it's you, I will give you three thousand kroner for it, take it off your hands.'

'Fine,' she said. Just like that, fine. She watched impatiently as he peeled the three banknotes from the warm, curved wad in his back pocket, then tucked them into her handbag without looking at them, and headed for the door.

'Wait,' he said. 'Don't you want a receipt?'

But she made a dismissive gesture with her hand, and the next minute she was gone, jumping into her car and pulling out into the midday traffic.

He watched from behind the window until she had turned the corner and disappeared before locking and bolting the door and drawing down the blind.

Then he ran back to his desk and shuffled frantically through his papers for his valuation book. He had not been mistaken. A piece of this pedigree could fetch as much as 75,000 kroner at auction. And then there was the intriguing gargoyle figure on the centre panel, something he had never seen before. The tallboy was bound to have provenance – only a matter of looking hard enough.

He fetched his brushes and rags and set to work. From a box of scraps, he cut tiny pieces of veneer and fixed them with glue, replacing the shards that had splintered away. Then, with a thick waxed crayon he had matched in colour to the flame mahogany, he filled the scratches. He checked that the drawers opened and closed smoothly, and carefully tacked into place the back panel where it had been damaged by the woman's rough handling.

Finally, he applied a thin layer of beeswax all across the chest and buffed it by hand till his shirt was soaked with sweat. By the time he was done, it was dark and the traffic had died down in the street outside.

When he had put away his tools and turned off the light, he stood for a moment in the dark and looked at the tallboy. Next to the other pieces of furniture in the shop, it felt alive and throbbing with energy, like a thoroughbred stallion among rocking horses.

Upstairs, he made a thorough online search for the demon motif on the front panel. He looked at hundreds of inlaid pictures of trees, flowers and figures, but none remotely resembled the gargoyle figure on the tallboy.

When he had exhausted all options, he rang a dealer in London who left him on hold for a long time as she searched through her papers and filing cabinets.

'I have something here, but it may not be related. There was this earl in the south-west of England a few centuries ago with a fondness for the macabre: body parts in specimen jars, maidens trapped behind walls, torture, that sort of thing. His coat of arms included a laughing, demonic figure. A bit like the one you're describing. Send me a photograph and I will let you know for sure.'

He thanked the dealer and hung up, having no intention whatsoever of sending her a picture.

'Nice try,' he said out loud, smiling at the thought that he himself would have done exactly the same, then somehow tried to get his colleague to sell him the piece cheaply under the pretence that it wasn't worth much.

He made a list of dealers that he was going to approach in the morning. If the woman in London had been right, there were plenty of bloodthirsty collectors out there who would be willing to part with a lot of money to get their hands on the tallboy.

After supper, he spent a pleasant evening in front of the television, browsing holiday brochures. A nice little winter break and there would still be plenty of money left over. He fell asleep early, his arms aching, his hands stained a deep brown.

He was woken by a loud knocking sound, or at least he thought he was. He lay in the dark, blinking at the ceiling and trying to work out if the sound had been part of his dream. But there it was again, an urgent rapping of knuckles on the front door downstairs.

His mind raced through the possibilities. Could it be the police? He was an honest man, mostly, but there was no accounting for his customers. Could the coffee table he had bought the day before have been stolen?

The knocking started up again. Surely, if it had been the police, they would have called out to him by now, ordered him to come and open the door.

The thought that hit him then was even worse. What if it was a disgruntled customer wanting his money back? What if the blonde woman had realised her mistake and sent someone to fetch the tallboy?

He tried to ignore it, but the knocking kept on, and it was getting louder. Though he pressed his hands to his ears, it was impossible to shut it out. It was the sort of urgent appeal that compelled you to respond, to obey, to take immediate action.

He got up, tiptoed down the stairs. The knocking was deafening now. He stood in the shadows of the hallway and glanced towards the back entrance, his heart hammering in his throat. There was still time to slip out, but the back door would only take him through to the yard, and what if there was someone waiting for him out there? He would be trapped and no one would hear him and come to his rescue.

He peered into the shop. All of a sudden he was afraid. The knocking was not coming from the front door; it was coming from the centre of the room. It was coming from the tallboy.

He held his ears. The knocking was unbearably loud, panicked and desperate. His heart was beating along with it, pounding on his ribcage. The sound was echoing inside his skull as though it had been hollowed out and a great bell made from it that would not stop ringing. He pulled at his hair, pulled at his pyjamas, tearing them off. And all the time that leprechaun, that gargoyle or devil inlaid in the wood, was glaring at him from the tallboy, mocking him.

It was as though someone was trapped behind the centre panel, as though he himself was trapped and knocking to get out.

He grasped at the panel with his fingers, tried to wedge a fingernail under the edge, to get purchase. He hammered on it with his fists, roaring at the noise to stop, to release him, to set him free.

In desperation, he ran back to the workshop, picked up a jimmy and tried to prise the panel off, but the jimmy kept slipping, and the panel wouldn't budge and in the end he was smashing the jimmy against the panel, and tears were running down his face at the damage he was doing, but still the knocking went on and on and on.

He guessed it must have stopped sometime towards morning. He woke on the shop floor in broad daylight, half-dressed and chilled to the bone, his head a tender lump of meat, his throat as dry as paper.

The tallboy loomed over him, ruined, his work the day before undone and all the pleasure from it vanished. He groaned at the thought of the woman, the dark rings under her eyes, the way she had practically run out of the shop.

There had been no elderly father, no old people's home, he saw that now.

He got to the jumble sale with less than an hour to spare. In the boot of his car, tossed in an old dust sheet, the tallboy shone like fire.

He saw the man coming, almost certainly a dealer, his eyes homing in on the tallboy from across the car park. He saw him feign disinterest, rummaging through cardboard boxes of bric-a-brac on the nearby stalls before sidling over with his hands in his pockets and nodding nonchalantly at the tallboy as though it was nothing.

'What have you got there?'

He told himself, Don't rush it now, before setting aside his crossword, getting up from his folding chair and moving towards the man, gesturing disarmingly and mustering his best smile.

'Just an old chest of drawers. It was my mother's, but we had to put her into a home, so . . .'

Detained

Clarissa knew something was wrong as soon as she emerged from customs. There was no sign of a driver holding a hand-written board with 'Miss Clarke' on it. The vast arrivals hall was deserted but for one other traveller, drifting like a solitary skater on a frozen lake.

Clarissa wheeled her suitcase to the exit, her high heels clacking resolutely on the tiled floor. But when the doors slid open, she felt a thousand icy pinpricks on her face. In the orange glare from the street light, the snow seemed to be falling horizontally.

The car park was a desolate tundra, the rows of vehicles covered by a thick white blanket. No sound could be heard but the wind howling across the snowdrifts. If there had ever been any taxis, they had been snapped up by the other passengers on the flight from Amsterdam.

As she stepped back inside, brushing snow off her coat, Clarissa felt a twist of indignation: for the world to grind to a halt because of a simple blizzard, and in Denmark of all places. Had these people never heard of snowploughs, or winter tyres?

She wiped her face dry with her hands and got out a mirror to check her eye make-up.

A security guard stood a little way off, looking out at the snow with his hands clasped at his back. Good, she thought, help at last. She walked over and tapped the man on the shoulder. He turned unhurriedly, and looked down at her with a mournful expression.

She opened her bag, started rummaging around for her purse and the address of the hotel.

'I want to leave,' she said. 'I have to be somewhere in the morning. Can you get me a taxi, please? I don't care how much it costs.'

Silence.

Clarissa looked up to find the security guard staring out of the window again.

'The snow,' he said after a while. 'It's a bad storm. All the roads are closed, no taxis.'

She considered tapping on his shoulder again, but something about his sloping back in the blue uniform jumper told her this would be pointless. His trousers were sagging, dragged down by a heavy set of keys clasped to one belt loop.

The other traveller, a middle-aged businessman in a dark suit and camel overcoat, carrying a holdall and some plastic bags, passed her on his orbit. Though he was a total stranger, Clarissa felt oddly comforted by his presence. Business travellers were a tribe, she had always thought. In airport lounges, taxi queues and hotel lifts, they would exchange little nods of recognition, like bikers on the open road.

She wondered if the man had also been on the flight from Amsterdam. She didn't remember seeing him earlier when she was waiting an eternity for her suitcase to appear on the baggage carousel. Perhaps the two of them could put their brains together and find some way out of here? She started towards him, but the man moved off.

Clarissa gave up on the security guard and the traveller and went to search for someone more cooperative. At the car-hire desks and bureaux de change, swivel chairs had been left at awkward angles. There was no one in sight. On the screens suspended from the ceiling, she noticed that the remaining arrivals of the night had been cancelled. Her flight from Amsterdam had been the last one in.

The departure lounge was equally abandoned, and all the shops were closed. In one window there was a pair of high-heeled red shoes: Italian leather, greasy and plump like ripe fruit, like lipstick for the feet. The sort of shoes she could never wear for work. The sort of shoes she never had an occasion to wear at all.

Clarissa sat down and tried to control her mounting panic. There was no one else in the entire airport but the unhelpful security guard and her aloof fellow traveller.

In her handbag, she found two plastic-wrapped biscuits from the plane and washed them down with the remainder of a bottle of tepid water, swallowing back tears. She wanted to strangle Tracy, her personal assistant, for booking the sales week in Amsterdam back to back with the Danish conference. Tracy, who would be at home in London now, watching the Friday chat shows. Clarissa would have to wait till Monday to have Tracy's head on a plate, and by then she would no longer be angry enough to enjoy it.

She had to get to her hotel. Roger, the newly appointed CEO, wouldn't like it if she wasn't there by first thing tomorrow, and Clarissa hated letting people down, particularly over something as inconsequential, surely, as snow in Denmark.

'Play your cards right with the Danes and you could be in line for director. You'll be one of the big boys then,' Roger had said.

It would mean more travel, and Clarissa would have to be based at the Hanover office. 'But we all have to pay our dues, Clarissa,' Roger had said.

Roger, who had joined the company at the same time as her and made it to the top, while she had got stuck in sales. Roger, who would be somewhere in Surrey now, making love to his beautiful young wife.

If it was Arctic weather outside, why was it so unbearably hot inside the terminal? Clarissa took off her coat. The synthetic lining made her hair stand on end. She hadn't closed an eye on the journey from Amsterdam and needed to sleep now, like the dead.

The security guard filed past, casting a pitying look in her direction. She decided to find a more private spot where she would be able to get a few hours' kip until the snow stopped and she could get a taxi. She found a couple of freestanding advertising screens that she managed to push open a little. Behind them was a carpeted area where she spread her coat on the floor and placed her suitcase and laptop in such a way that she would wake up if someone tried to take them. Then she wrapped her arms around her handbag and closed her eyes, wondering if any amount of sleep could cure the kind of tiredness she was suffering from.

Sometime later she became aware of a loud scratching noise. She opened her eyes, blinking, and saw that there was a man looking at her.

'I'm sorry, did I wake you?' he said.

Clarissa recognised the other traveller, the businessman she had seen in the arrivals hall. He was sitting cross-legged on the floor about two metres away from her. She sat up. 'What are you doing?'

'Perhaps I should be the one asking you that?' he said in perfect English with some indefinable European accent.

Clarissa caught a whiff of sweat from her clothes. Her body felt creased and sore, her hair flat and clingy. She needed a good, hot shower, fresh clothes and a strong cup of tea.

The man carried on drawing. The scratching noise came from a stick of charcoal, which he was moving furiously across a large sketchpad in his lap.

'There's a whole empty airport out there,' she said, tucking in her shirt. 'Why do you have to sit right here?'

'This is my space. I was here long before you,' he said.

'Don't be absurd. No one owns this space.'

Clarissa noticed now that the man's shirt was dirty around the collar. His camel coat was torn in places, there were shiny patches on the knees of his suit, and his bag was held together by a brown leather belt. The man looked at Clarissa and smiled so widely she could see all his back teeth were missing.

'Who are you?' she asked throatily, her anger replaced by prickling fear.

This was no fellow business traveller. The main thing now was to keep calm, keep him talking. 'Where are you from?' she said.

'Here.'

'You're from the airport?'

Clarissa laughed and the man joined in, continuing to laugh long after she had stopped.

'Yes,' he said.

Clarissa sat up, clutching her handbag.

'But you can't be living here, it's not possible,' she said, looking discreetly for her suitcase. It was safe behind her.

'But I do. For the time being, at least, I do.'

'You'll get yourself arrested.'

'No one notices a businessman in an airport.'

'I could tell the security guard.'

'Svend, you mean? He doesn't give damn about anything. Not since his wife left him.'

'But why live here?' she asked.

'It's warm. There are toilets, showers, food. I am only staying for a while, until I decide where to go next. They say Heathrow is nice.'

Clarissa changed position, wrapping her arms around her knees. She could feel the man continue to stare at her.

'I used to sell insurance,' he said. 'Then, one day, I decided I didn't want to do it any more. I disappeared. What's the matter? You think you couldn't do the same?' he said.

'Of course I couldn't. People would miss me. For a start, I'm first speaker at a big conference in Aalborg tomorrow morning,' she said, glancing at her suitcase again.

Her presentation, *A Vision for the 21st Century: Integrated Business Software,* was in there on a memory stick together with her laptop and the folder with the signed contracts from Amsterdam.

'So you don't turn up – so what?'

'I'm very good at my job; the company needs me.'

'They'll get someone else tomorrow.'

'Not like me they won't.'

'You think you're so important. I'll tell you something: no one will miss you. They'll talk about it for a few days, and then the weeks will pass, the months, the years, and they will forget.'

Clarissa felt her cheeks glow. 'Look mister, whoever you are,' she said, jabbing a finger at the man. 'You've no right to make assumptions. You don't know the first thing about me.'

'OK, let's see now. I know you're not married.'

'Says who?'

'You're not wearing a ring.'

'Lots of married people don't wear rings.'

'So I'm wrong?'

Clarissa looked down.

'And you're tired, but you think that you can't stop whatever it is that's making you tired, or something terrible will happen.'

'And you have it all sorted out, do you? Look at the state of you,' she spat.

'I'll go some day. Until then, I stay here. I'm in no hurry,' the man stared at her until she had to look away.

He went back to his drawing and started singing quietly, retreating into some world of his own. He didn't seem to notice when Clarissa noisily gathered up her things and left. She walked down the stairs and away to the far corner of the building.

She didn't often have a chance to think about her life, or maybe she didn't want to. On Boxing Day the year before, she had left her mother's house first thing to go into work and finish a sales pitch that had to be ready before the New Year. On the way, she had called a younger member of her team who had recently become a father, and asked him to come in and help her. He had told her to 'get a life' and hung up. She had sacked him the following week, but it had made her cry.

She had worked hard to get where she was. It would be madness to give it up now, just before she was due to get the executive position that was rightfully hers. Besides, she liked her job. She couldn't recall a time when she was happy doing anything else.

Clarissa thought of the strange man who lived in the airport and all the people from all over the world he would be watching every day, people like her, coming and going. What had he seen? What had he been drawing? She lay back on a bench, her brain racing. Many metres above, she saw her own reflection in the ceiling, a tiny speck in a white emptiness.

Everything felt strange all of a sudden.

Hours later, as the world outside the terminal grew visible in the grey morning light, the airport gradually filled up with travellers anxious to make their connections. It was as if last night's storm had never happened, yet everything felt different to Clarissa, somehow transformed.

As she got up, something fell to the floor. It was a piece of paper torn from a sketchbook, a charcoal drawing with a furious mess of black lines. She had to hold it with her arms outstretched to make sense of it. Then she recognised herself sleeping, a deep frown creasing her forehead, her eyes closed and her mouth slightly open, with the corners turned down in despair. She was hugging her handbag as though it were an ice float and she was drowning in a vast, dark sea.

She looked around for the man, but there were too many people in the airport now, people carrying holdalls and plastic bags, dressed in suits and brown overcoats, all looking as though they had somewhere to be urgently. The traveller could be any one of them.

It felt right when she walked to the nearest toilet and opened her suitcase, took out the memory stick with the presentation for the Aalborg conference and placed it in the sanitary bin. She tore up and flushed the Amsterdam sales contracts down the loo one by one, then pushed each of her vast collection of business cards through a drain cover in the floor. She drowned her mobile phone in the cistern and watched page by page of her diary getting sucked into a ventilation shaft.

After that it seemed like no big deal to walk across the busy airport floor and buy a pair of red shoes, shiny like waxed apples. She put them on straight away, dropped her practical heels in a rubbish bin, and strode towards the exit, imagining a room full of Danish executives looking at their watches and the empty space on the podium with the card marked *Miss Clarissa Clarke, United Kingdom.*

When she stepped outside, her red-shod feet like blood in the snow, the light was blinding.

The Crying

There is an area of old Copenhagen, close to the harbour and the royal castle, where the population thins dramatically at night. Where once there were families and servants, now there are lawyers and bankers. In the evenings, when they leave for the suburbs, the place falls almost silent.

This was what Jens loved most about his new apartment: that he had the neighbourhood to himself when he returned from the office, the footsteps of his brogues echoing between the tall, empty mansions.

Looking up at the windows of Amalienborg Palace, he would imagine Queen Margrethe, seated in the dark by the desk at which she gave her New Year's address to the nation, gazing out at the city.

Jens particularly loved the autumn, when Copenhagen

turned grey and gold and the streets closed in, hurrying you towards the light and warmth of the indoors. Crossing the cobbled courtyard to his building, he would start running, then bound two steps at a time to the third floor. Inside the apartment, stroking Mortensen, his tabby cat, he became a wealthy merchant, counting his doorknobs and keys like pieces of silver.

The rooms smelled of boot polish, cedar and coffee, evoking in him images of important dinner parties and secret affairs. If he sat very still, Jens could hear the groaning of the 300-year-old timbers and he thought of the building, not as dead with its sloping floors, bowing windows and cracked walls, but as a living, breathing thing.

His colleagues thought he lived in the suburbs like them. No one knew the truth, not even his parents in their bungalow across the sea on the other side of Denmark, but then they knew nothing. As far as they were concerned, he was working in Greenland on a remote research station.

All day, as he entered figures into columns, Jens savoured his secret that he owned a palace with tall ceilings and more rooms than he could ever afford to furnish.

The apartment itself had not come free, of course. Such places rarely became available, and the asking price had far exceeded his modest means. But the first time he saw it, he knew he had to have it, whatever it took, whatever he would have to do.

The apartment belonged to an old widow who had lived there for more than sixty years.

'Will she take an offer?' he asked the estate agent.

'You must be joking. I have a dozen buyers interested,' said the agent, his torso so inflated that his chin appeared to be resting on his chest.

'We'll see what she has to say about that,' said Jens.

The agent looked directly at him for the first time then, his eyes narrowing behind his half-moon glasses. Jens knew what those eyes saw: someone unworthy of prime Copenhagen, someone more suited for a yellow-brick block south of the city.

'You can't call the vendor directly, you know,' the agent said.

'Wouldn't dream of it,' Jens replied.

It wasn't hard to get the telephone number. Seated on her best sofa, sipping perfumed tea from a china cup, Mrs Andersen talked a great deal about her move to the care home in the countryside. Jens knew that all he had to do was to listen and wait.

As the grandfather clock in the corner struck the second hour, Mrs Andersen went on to talk about her late husband. Apparently, she had never seen his feet naked before he lay dead on the mortuary slab. Even in their most intimate moments, he would not remove his socks. Again and again, Mrs Andersen returned to this absurd fact, as though it had shocked her more profoundly than the man keeling over at breakfast some twenty years ago. Jens stayed silent, all the while picturing himself walking through Mrs Andersen's majestic rooms.

'I like your apartment,' he told her when she tired of talking. 'It feels so, I don't know, homely. But the thing is Mrs Andersen ...'

'Ingrid.'

'Ingrid. The thing is, since my parents both passed away in the accident, I have had rather a lot of debt to settle and the proceeds from the house barely covers it, and this money is all I have left. But I really need somewhere to live, if only I could afford this place ...'

'Slow down, dear. Your parents were killed, you said?'

A few days later the estate agent called to inform Jens in a clipped voice that it would appear Mrs Andersen had chosen to accept his offer, though it was so far below market value as to be indecent.

On the day Jens moved in, he couldn't stop laughing. He danced across the naked floorboards and opened the doors wide to all the rooms. When he had finished unpacking his meagre belongings, he sat for a long while on one of the windowsills and watched the sun set behind the roofs of the city.

Two months later, when he was demolishing the first of the apartment's antique wooden panels, the memory of the happiness of that first day felt to Jens like a physical pain.

It had all started with the crying.

When he first heard it, in the middle of the night, it meant little more than a distant police siren, nothing to do with him. The crying, a persistent but remote wail, wove its way into his dreams as he went back to sleep.

The next morning, he would have forgotten all about it, had Mortensen not refused to come out from under his bed.

Then on another night it happened again, but this time it was much louder, an indignant, full-lung bawl of the kind that urges you to respond without delay. It was late and Jens was in the kitchen, frying an egg. He walked around, trying to locate the sound. It appeared to come from one of the bedrooms at the end of the long corridor that ran through the apartment like the backbone of a great whale, but when he turned on the light, the room was empty and silent.

Later he found Mortensen hiding under his bed again.

The crying came from an infant. It was a muffled sound, as if behind a wall or inside a box or under a pillow, and it always stopped when Jens felt he was getting near to locating it.

He racked his brain for clues. The first two floors of the building were occupied by a firm of solicitors. On the second floor was Miss Vagn, an old spinster who had owned her apartment for at least as long as Mrs Andersen. He lived on the third floor and the apartment above his, the last in the property, was empty. Its owners, a retired banker and his wife, lived most of the year in Geneva, which meant that at night, when the solicitors went home, only Miss Vagn and he remained.

Jens considered for a few days the possibility that the sound was being carried over on the wind from one of the neighbouring properties. One weekend, he went out in the rain and searched the entire street and its backyards for signs of prams, tricycles or anything that might belong to a family, but there was nothing of the kind. The only time Jens ever saw children, with their brightly coloured raincoats and loud, irrational manners, was when school excursions walked by on their way to watch the changing of the Queen's guard. Occasionally, women or couples would pass by the building pushing prams, but never at night, never when the crying happened.

The crying burrowed under Jens's skin till he could no longer function. All night he would lie awake waiting for it to begin, then furiously search the apartment. In the morning he would arrive at the tax office looking haggard, spending most of the day asleep at his desk or thinking about the crying. One day, his supervisor, a woman in her fifties whose only son had recently left home to go to university, came over and bent down low by his work station. She was so close, Jens could see the greasy fingermarks on her glasses and the blonde moustache on her upper lip.

'Are you all right, Jens? You are looking very pale,' she said in a barely audible voice.

'Just a little tired, Tove,' said Jens. His supervisor, her

bosom bouncing under her knitted jumper, liked being called by her first name. 'In fact, if you must know, they think I might have cancer,' he added.

'My God. What sort?' said Tove, placing one hand on his shoulder. It felt heavy and damp through the fabric of his shirt.

'They don't know, yet. I'm having some tests, but it doesn't look good,' said Jens, shaking his head a little and staring at the pot plant on Tove's desk. He had often felt like biting into its glossy, swollen leaves.

Tove wouldn't hear of him staying on at work, but ordered him to go home and take it easy, which he tried his best to do.

However, he rested even less than before, as there was now no respite from the perpetual listening and waiting for the crying to begin. It was an instrument of torture, drilling its way into Jens's brain and lodging itself there so that he could hear it even when the apartment was quiet.

Throughout the ordeal, Mortensen had stayed aloof and absent, keeping himself, so it seemed increasingly to Jens, deliberately scarce in the few days after each incident of the crying. Come to think of it, Jens had never seen Mortensen when the crying had actually occurred. This thought occupied him a great deal and, as the days went by, Jens started looking at Mortensen with suspicion. He took to bringing the cat to bed with him each night, holding the creature tight to his chest.

'You stay right here, and you and I will be just fine,' he would say.

But Mortensen would look away with his beautiful green eyes, as though embarrassed on Jens's behalf. He had always been a particularly arrogant cat, only just tolerating Jens's awkward affection. This, though part of the reason why he was so fond of Mortensen, drove Jens to a crazed distraction.

His attempt to keep the cat in sight at all times was unsuccessful. In the early hours Jens would drift off to sleep and by the time the crying started the cat had long since slunk away from his slackened grip.

One night, as Jens was woken up by the crying, the thought came to his delirious mind that the crying was no infant at all, but the mating call of a cat, a cat not unlike Mortensen. In fact, was this not the cry of Mortensen himself? Jens felt relief at this thought. He got up calmly and walked through the apartment, quickly finding Mortensen in the corner of one of the rooms. The cat had its back up, baring its teeth in a blood-chilling tiger growl. Jens grabbed it hard around the neck with both hands.

It was surprisingly effortless, like squeezing a wet sock, and it came with no satisfaction at all. When Mortensen's body went limp, Jens knew, if only with one corner of his fevered mind, that there was no way the crying had come from the cat.

When Jens woke up the next day there was a message

on the answering machine from Tove: if he needed to talk to someone, then he knew where to find her. After listening to the message he wrapped Mortensen's body in old newspapers and a plastic bag and went down to the basement to place it in one of the dustbins. He took a shower, shaved off three weeks' growth of beard and put on a fresh shirt. Then he walked down one flight of stairs, hesitating with his finger on the ivory bell. There was a sign on the door with a picture of an Alsatian and the words *Beware of the dog.*

Miss Vagn opened immediately, almost tripping over the threshold, as if she had been waiting just inside, hovering with her faced pressed to the spyhole.

Her eyes, grotesquely distorted by thick glasses, peered out at Jens sideways. Her hair, most likely a wig, judging by its faint synthetic sheen, was black, her face a pasty beige on which her none-too-accurately painted lips floated like a glob of strawberry jam.

Jens knew straight away that Ms Vagn was going to like him; women like her always did.

'Jens Bruun,' he said. 'I live upstairs?'

'Yes?' She stared up at him trustingly. Ingrid must have told her about him buying the apartment.

'The thing is, Miss Vagn. There's this noise I've been hearing at night. A crying baby, and I wondered if it ... I wondered if you might know something about it?'

'A baby?' Miss Vagn shook her head. 'There's no baby

here. I don't know anything about a baby.' Her voice was a little too loud, with the peculiar intonation of people in old films.

'Are you sure? I tell you, Miss Vagn, that I most definitely have heard a baby crying somewhere in or near my apartment. And you have really heard nothing of the sort, and know nothing about it?' he said.

'I am sorry, no.'

On seeing him disappointed, Miss Vagn opened the door wider. Inside the apartment, an old carriage clock struck the quarter-hour.

'Do come in and have a glass of port with me,' she said.

'What about the . . . ?' said Jens, gesturing at the sign with the picture of the Alsatian.

'Oh,' she said. 'Died 1993.'

Jens was glad about that. Dogs, like small children, upset him with their overwhelming behaviour. Inside Miss Vagn's apartment, as she retired to the kitchen, the first thing he noticed was that the place was identical to his own, which ought not to have surprised him, but did. Furthermore, it was a good deal more impressive, as Miss Vagn had no shortage of expensive things.

Miss Vagn returned with a bottle and two small glasses on a tray and beckoned him to take a seat in the sofa. It seemed odd, frankly suspicious, to Jens that she was not curious in the slightest about the crying.

'*Skål*,' she said, lifting her glass and knocking the

contents back in one go. Jens noticed how the empty glass shook in her hand.

Strong and sweet, the port gave Jens the sort of nausea that spreads like an ache from the top of the head, but Miss Vagn filled his glass again before he could stop her. She was leaning towards him from her armchair next to the sofa, so close he could smell her perfume and the sickly brown powder that caked her face like dough. Her lips were parted a little, revealing her yellow teeth. Jens shuddered.

They might have been sitting like that for ages or merely a few seconds. Lack of sleep had turned Jens's vision into a naked, flickering light bulb, intermittently illuminating Miss Vagn's bottle-end glasses. Across the gap in their years he heard her loneliness and physical longing, like a calling out, like a crying, and the madness overtook him once again.

As he reached out for her throat she didn't struggle; it was as if she welcomed his hands there, as if any touch was better than none, which infuriated him even more.

Strangling Miss Vagn was no harder than strangling Mortensen, nor did it bring more relief.

Jens considered her body for a while then decided to leave it. It was unlikely to be found, considering no visitors ever called anywhere on the upper floors. As he walked back up the stairs to his apartment, he thought, I have killed a cat and a human being for no reason at all.

That night, when the crying started up again, Jens

himself cried with the bitterness of someone who can have no solace and no satisfaction. Into the crying he rolled all the unfairness of his life, and he and the ghostly baby wailed in unison till he did not know which sound came from the infant and which from himself.

It was the next day that he started on the wall panels in the smallest bedroom at the end of the corridor.

That morning Jens had woken with a new resolve. First he rang work, telling Tove that he'd been diagnosed with a rare form of brain cancer. He was flying to the US for treatment that same afternoon and she should not expect him back at work for some considerable time. Then he went down to the basement and picked up an axe from the boiler room.

The crying began at twilight and Jens walked calmly through all the rooms, following the sound, which came – he was certain of it now – from behind the walls in the little room overlooking the back yard. As he cleaved and tore off the panels one by one until only the skeletal timbers remained, how good it felt finally to be doing something. And when he found there was nothing to see in the little room, he started on the next room and the one after that, growing more determined with each strike of the axe not to finish till everything had been torn down and exposed, if necessary to move through the whole building, never stopping till he had silenced the crying.

The Last Tenant

Jan Vettergren stopped typing, looked up from his laptop and sniffed the air. The smell was back, boiled cabbage and fish. This was what you got with old buildings, little quirks and peculiarities. Jan guessed the woodwork had somehow absorbed the odours of the meals that had been cooked there over the years. There were no private apartments in the neighbourhood any more, and no restaurants: nothing else to explain the smell.

He went back to work, trying to concentrate on the press release he was writing. The client was expecting it in the morning. He would have to stay till it was done, but his mind kept drifting back to what the place must have been like once. He loved the way the floorboards had been worn down in the middle of the stairs, the creaking doors, the panelled windows, bowing in their frames. And to think that it was all his.

He had thought it was a joke when they told him the price. It was all he could do to keep a straight face as he asked for a discount. The owner had given in surprisingly fast, letting Jan have the whole building for next to nothing.

People lacked imagination; that was why no one else wanted it. They couldn't see past the tarnished walls, the graffiti and the windows on the ground floor, boarded up with perforated steel.

Jan had no problem with any of that. As soon as his fledgling PR agency had made enough money, he was going to fix up the other offices in the building and rent them out, make a fortune. In fact, he might give up PR altogether and branch off into property. Who knew how many buildings like this one were standing empty across central Copenhagen?

Jan reckoned the former owner would kick himself when he realised what he had thrown away.

They had chosen the best office for themselves, the fifth floor with the lovely original tiled stoves and the views over the red rooftops and golden church spires of old Copenhagen. One weekend, they had painted layer upon layer of pure white over the soiled wallpaper, and scrubbed and varnished the floors. The dark woods set off their modern furniture beautifully.

It was obvious no one had used the office for years. In what used to be the lounge, they had found a newspaper from 1989 tucked behind a telex machine, a beige monstrosity the size of a small fridge. On a desk, among faded carbon copies of final demands, a once-white telephone had aged to ivory, its receiver suspended in mid-air.

Strange that the previous tenants hadn't bothered tidying up after themselves, or taken their office furniture away and sold it. Jan reckoned they must have had to close down in a hurry: bankruptcy, perhaps, or a court case.

There was no trace of the mess now. Just the little things that made Jan and his colleagues frown. Like the cooking smells. Or the sudden and inexplicable draughts. Or the fact that the white paint persisted in coming off the walls in long jagged flakes, revealing the grimy wallpaper beneath.

Quirks, that was all it was, idiosyncrasies, the sort of character people were willing to pay good money for. Jan had told the company accountant as much, but Margit was not convinced. She had worked up some crackpot theory that 'something or someone' was intent on expelling them. Like the Monday morning recently when they had come in to find that an unpleasant dark stain, removed from the reception floor on the Friday, had reappeared. Or when their newly mounted modern paintings had come off the walls during the night, each and every wire snapped.

None of the others had wanted to work alone in the office after that.

'We're not wanted here,' Margit had said.

The thought of the melodramatic expression on her face

when she said that made him laugh out loud, but his voice rang strangely in the empty room, and there was something else now, something that made him stop and listen. He closed his eyes, tried to filter out the hum from his laptop and the night buses spraying slush on the main road.

There was definitely *something* there, little regular creaks in the corridor. His mind raced through the options: one of his staff had come back for something, a cat had found its way in, or the central heating was making the floorboards expand and crack.

'Hello?' he shouted. 'Anyone there?'

Nothing.

There was another possibility, of course: squatters. It made sense, a property standing empty for so long in a prime neighbourhood. As he strained to hear, he made a mental note to call in a security firm in the morning.

The little creaks started up again, louder this time. They sounded a lot like footsteps now. He looked around for a weapon, picked up an umbrella and put it down again. Considered a cardboard tube holding proofs of new posters for Copenhagen's City Bikes, but thought better of it. Finally, he settled on a magnum of champagne someone had brought to their launch party. He held it like a club.

The corridor was empty. Where the white paint had come off in scrolls, you could see pale ovals and rectangles on the old wallpaper, the shapes of pictures that had once hung there.

The meeting room was deserted and dark, the plasma screen for their video conferences still in its box and stacked against one wall. After the incident with the paintings, no one had felt much like trying to mount it. Jan told himself that once he had investigated the strange noise, he would unpack the screen and hang it, using the power drill and four-inch bolts he had brought from home.

In his partner's office, there was still a sheet draped over the desk, though they had managed to clean up most of the mess. It was unfortunate what had happened to Kristoffer. They still had no idea how the screws holding the heavy ceiling lamp directly above his chair had managed to work themselves free from the plaster. Bad luck that he had been sitting there at the time.

Jan looked inside the galley kitchen where they kept their Italian coffee machine and the microwave and their personal mugs, all eight of them lined up on the counter. Jan doubted Kristoffer would have much use of his now.

The kitchen was cold, though the window was closed. The smell of cabbage and fish was stronger here. Perhaps there was something rotten in the bin? He was about to open the lid and have a look inside when he was startled by the lift starting up, pulling noisily on its cables in the shaft on the other side of the wall.

He was the only one who used the ancient contraption. The others were put off by its narrow dimensions and the way it sometimes ran by itself or stalled on their floor, endlessly opening and closing the doors on the empty car. The date of the last service was 16 October 1991, according to the signed engineer's report fixed to the wall inside.

Jan went out on the landing and looked at the old-fashioned half-moon display above the lift. The car had descended all the way to the cellar. He reached out for the call button, but changed his mind and turned towards the stairs, lest he gave himself away to the intruder.

The stairwell was shabby and poorly lit with a faint, bittersweet smell of Bakelite and cigars. Light rectangles on the linoleum showed where there had once been doormats at the entrance to each apartment. Signs announced the names of businesses long gone: an independent record label, a reflexologist, a temping agency. One door was blackened by soot, and another had been gutted by what looked like an axe, leaving the wood in long, jagged splinters.

Jan bent down and looked through the gap. On the hallway floor inside lay a pile of unopened mail. The envelopes looked green and fuzzy, as though made from felt or some organic material. He recoiled as he realised they were covered in mould. A trail of dark stains led off into the murky depths of the apartment.

He continued down the stairs, almost stumbling in fright when his phone went off in his pocket. It was Margit.

'What is it?' he snapped, annoyed with himself for being so jittery.

'Where are you?'

'At work, someone has to be.'

'If I were you, I'd leave at once,' she said. 'I've done some research. There was this tenant once, back when they turned the block into offices. They say that he refused to leave.'

'Blah, blah, blah,' Jan said. 'I'm not listening.'

He walked over to the window. Across the snow-speckled courtyard he could see the larger and more imposing office building that fronted the road. It had been refurbished a few years ago, the old features ripped out and replaced by New York loft-style bricks and beams. The open-plan floors were lit up, showing row upon row of white desks and chairs.

It was strange to think that where suited advertising executives now spent their days sipping cappuccinos, hundreds of men, women and children had once lived together, crammed into tiny apartments, with a shared outside privy. Must have been freezing in winter, Jan thought.

Margit was still talking when he put the phone back to his ear: 'Kristoffer may never be able to return to work. It took them the best part of a day to remove the shards of glass from his scalp and face.'

Jan had heard enough. 'Margit, if you want to keep working for me, I suggest you forget this superstitious nonsense. I'm hanging up now.'

'Wait, where are you exactly? What's that echo?' he heard Margit say before he ended the call and continued down the stairs.

Nothing happened when he flicked the light switch to the cellar. He hesitated on the steps, weary of the dark. Years ago, people would have done their laundry down there in great steaming vats, pegging their sheets on lines strung across the courtyard. There was a smell of wet cement. Somewhere in the darkness below, a tap was dripping.

He held up his phone and descended the steps very slowly, struggling to see in the foggy blue light from the display. Towards the back of the cellar, there was a row of lock-up storage rooms, one for each of the twelve apartments. He pointed the light through the grilles, saw a rusty bicycle, stacks of wooden crates, an old pram.

His grip tightened around the neck of the champagne bottle as he reached the lock-up belonging to their office. Slowly he lifted his phone and shone the light inside. Nothing, just stacks of old newspapers, discarded lampshades, a mattress and bits of worn carpet.

It took a while for his heartbeat to return to normal. Then he got angry. Someone had deliberately sent him on a wild goose chase to the cellar. He had thought himself on an intruder's tail, when all along they had only wanted him out of the way so they could clear out the office computers and TV screens.

He raced up the stairs two steps at a time, but he was too late, someone had been in his office already. The papers on his desk had been knocked to the floor and were fluttering all over the place.

'Show yourself, whoever you are!' he shouted.

One of the windows had been opened, filling the room with icy, wet air. The pane kept slamming back against the frame, like someone knocking urgently on a door. Jan remembered that there was a narrow ledge outside the window, big enough to hold a man. He pretended to leave the room, deliberately making a loud noise as he did so and switching off the light.

'Don't make me come and find you,' he shouted down the hall.

Then he tiptoed back into the room, the bottle of champagne raised high above his head. No one was going to put Jan Vettergren off; no one was going to stop him from doing exactly as he pleased with a property that was his by rights.

Perplexingly, the ledge was empty. At least he thought it was. He had to climb out of the window completely before he could be certain.

The bottle fell first. There was a long silence before it smashed on the cobbles in the yard far below. With an instinctive reaction, Jan leant forward to catch it, his hand grabbing fistfuls of air.

There was a brief moment before he lost his fight against the greater force pushing him forward, a split second in which he saw exactly what would happen: they would find him on the cobbles in the morning, surrounded by glass from the broken champagne bottle. It would look like an accident, like high jinks gone disastrously wrong.

No one would listen to Margit, a middle-aged bean counter with an overactive imagination. With neither Kristoffer nor himself around to run things, the lawyers would wind up the PR company and, eventually, the property would change hands again, as yet another buyer with a keen eye for a bargain succumbed to its charms: *Unique historic property in the heart of Copenhagen, bags of potential, a diamond in the rough.*

At the time it had not seemed important, but Jan recalled now how vigorously the previous owner had shaken his hand, how quickly he had headed for the door.

As the ground rushed towards him, he could hear the window high above slamming and opening, slamming and opening, like cruel, slow-handed applause.

Acknowledgements

Thanks to Jeremy Osborne and Sweet Talk Productions without whom many of these stories would not have come into being. *Last Train to Helsingør, The Music Box, The Chanterelles of Østvig, The Light from Dead Stars, Conning Mrs Vinterberg, The Bird in the Cage, The Climbing Rose, The Wailing Girl, Room Service, The Suitcase, The Tallboy, Detained* and *The Last Tenant* were previously produced by Sweet Talk for BBC Radio 4, and The Crying was first printed by *Mslexia*. Thanks to Sarah and Kate Beal at Muswell Press for giving this collection life, and to Kate Quarry for her astute editing. Thanks also to Helen Pike, William Weinstein and Jeff Walkden for being my first readers, and to Frederik and Jules for making it all worthwhile. Finally, thanks to my late grandmothers in and around whose homes in Copenhagen I spent long school holidays lost in my imagination. While some locations in these stories may be real, all characters and events are entirely fictional, and any mistakes my own.

Heidi Amsinck, a writer and journalist born in Copenhagen, spent many years covering Britain for the Danish press, including a spell as London Correspondent for the broadsheet daily Jyllands-Posten.

She has written numerous short stories for radio, including the three-story sets Danish Noir, Copenhagen Confidential and Copenhagen Curios, all produced by Sweet Talk for BBC Radio 4.

A graduate of the MA in Creative Writing at Birkbeck, University of London, Heidi lives in Surrey. She was previously shortlisted for the VS Pritchett Memorial Prize. *Last Train to Helsingør* is her first published collection of stories.